LOGAN'S LIGHT

Heroes for Hire, Book 6

Dale Mayer

Books in This Series:

Books in the SEALs of Honor Series:

LOGAN'S LIGHT: HEROES FOR HIRE, BOOK 6
Dale Mayer
Valley Publishing

ISBN-13: 978-1-773360-37-9
Print Edition

Back Cover

Welcome to Logan's Light, book 6 in Heroes for Hire, reconnecting readers with the unforgettable men from SEALs of Honor in a new series of action packed, page turning romantic suspense that fans have come to expect from USA TODAY Bestselling author Dale Mayer.

Logan heads to Boston on an intel mission. His investigation plunges him and his partner into the deep dark world of human trafficking.

The last thing Alina remembers is having coffee at the cafe in her hospital where she works. She woke up tied up in a strange apartment. Her world as she knew it gone... possibly forever.

Now they're on the run together. Time is against them. There's a quota to be made, and the traffickers aren't going to let Alina stay free if they can help it.

Unfortunately, she's not the only victim. The hunt is on... for the traffickers and their other victims... before it's too late.

Sign up to be notified of all Dale's releases here!

http://dalemayer.com/category/blog/

Your Free Book Awaits!

KILL OR BE KILLED

Part of an elite SEAL team, Mason takes on the dangerous jobs no one else wants to do – or can do. When he's on a mission, he's focused and dedicated. When he's not, he plays as hard as he fights.

Until he meets a woman he can't have but can't forget. Software developer, Tesla lost her brother in combat and has no intention of getting close to someone else in the military. Determined to save other US soldiers from a similar fate, she's created a program that could save lives. But other countries know about the program, and they won't stop until they get it – and get her.

Time is running out ... For her ... For him ... For them ...

DOWNLOAD a *__complimentary__* copy of MASON? Just tell me where to send it!

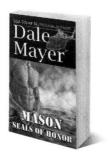

http://dalemayer.com/sealsmason/

Chapter 1

LOGAN REDDING DRESSED quickly for the job he was heading out to this morning, but Levi had yet to give him any details. In fact, the text had come through just before midnight. Logan had grabbed as much sleep as he could, then showered, shaved, packed and now he was ready to go. He entered the dining room to find six other team members already in place, Conversation died when he approached. "Good morning."

With a full cup of coffee, he sat beside them. "Levi, what's the job?"

"You and Harrison are heading to Boston. Four men held on suspicion of human trafficking were released—not enough evidence to hold them—and disappeared underground. The detective who hauled them in knows Jackson, who then called me privately. He asked if we could take a day or two to consider the case. It'll be pro bono. Detective James Easterly says something was rotten with those men and is afraid it's a much bigger issue, but he can't find any proof. He's been pulled off the case due to budget concerns and manpower shortages. He doesn't know Jackson has called me."

"We've budgeted forty-eight hours for this," Ice said. "Hopefully that's more than enough to sort it out."

"It's basically an intel-gathering mission." Levi lifted the folder and added, "I have names, backgrounds, and pictures of the suspects' faces. Jason Markham, Lance Haverstock, Barry Ferguson, and Bill Morgan. All deemed to be leaders in a human trafficking ring."

Harrison nodded. "We'll check out the men, and we won't do anything major. I suppose in that folder you have a few addresses of friends, family, or businesses that they're known to frequent—or ideas about where these guys may have gone to ground—so we'll casually walk around and observe. See if we find anything of importance. If we don't, well, it is what it is." He shrugged. "We won't even be official. Hell, we both have friends and family there. Logan can visit his friends, and I'll go check on my sister-in-law," Harrison continued cheerfully. "Besides Logan and I are getting seriously housebound. We need to get out. The *love boat* is a little bit much to handle right now."

Levi glared at him.

But Harrison's good humor was irrepressible. He grinned at Levi and said, "You know what I mean, Levi. A whole lot of cooing and sexy stuff is going on around here."

Katina reached across the table, grabbed Harrison's hand and said, "That's okay. We understand you're feeling left out and lonely. Maybe you'll find somebody special on this trip."

Harrison pulled away his hand, groaning under everyone's laughter.

Logan lifted his hand to share a high five with Harrison. "Perfect. I'm ready to go."

Harrison jumped to his feet. "Give me two minutes, and I'll meet you in the garage."

Sienna walked in. "Seats are still available on the flights out of Houston later this morning," she said. "I've reserved two." She turned to Levi. "Who's going?"

Levi motioned at Harrison and Logan. "Book the tickets for these two. Returning three days from now."

Sienna smiled, filled her coffee and said, "Be back in a few minutes then." She walked out as Harrison bolted behind her, calling out, "Make mine the window seat. Logan gets the aisle."

Logan could hear the two of them wrangling as they left the dining room.

"Watch your backs," Levi warned Logan. "It might look like a bullshit mission, but these guys weren't picked up in the first place without good reason."

Logan looked at Levi and said, "Are we talking kidnapping? Murder? Human trafficking within US soil or being shipped overseas?"

"All of it," Levi said. "You both be careful. We can be in the air and at your side within six hours at most. But that's still six you have to handle on your own."

Logan nodded as he walked into the kitchen. Alfred was making breakfast, his usual sausage and bacon entrées. He glanced at Logan and said, "It'll be ready in about ten minutes."

Logan nodded. "We'll probably stick around then. But we'll have to eat and run."

Logan returned to the sidebar in the dining room, filled his coffee cup and sat again. He had more questions, but the conversation had already moved on. Levi shoved the folder toward him. Logan opened it to find files inside—damn slim ones, at that—for the four men they would be looking for. He quickly read all the documents, finding nothing there.

He closed the folder and shoved it toward Levi. "I gather we'll take a copy when we leave?"

"Sienna is putting that together."

Logan nodded.

Then Alfred came in with a platter of toast and hash browns. "Tell Harrison to get down here for breakfast."

Logan sent a quick text to Harrison.

By the time Alfred had dished out the rest of the food, and Logan's plate had been filled, Harrison showed up. He dropped the paperwork beside Logan and said, "These are our flights and bookings, plus our copy of the file." He glanced at Levi. "Considering this is a pro bono job, do you want us to bunk with friends and family?"

"We'll book you in a hotel so we're sure you have a place."

Logan finished eating, and with Harrison at his side, they made quick good-byes and hopped into one of the trucks.

By now Levi had quite a fleet of vehicles. They often used a small truck for quick trips in and out of town, although it'd be a forty-five-minute drive to the airport. They would leave this one at the long-term airport parking while they were gone for the next few days. No sense in tying up somebody else's time to drop them off and pick them up.

At the airport, they cleared security in time to board straight onto the plane.

When they landed in Boston four hours later, they stepped outside the airport and stood, gazing at a misty afternoon, gray and cloudy. Logan looked over at Harrison and said, "Let's grab the rental car and get to the hotel."

At the rental office, they completed the paperwork and walked to the parking lot to locate the midsize vehicle.

Logan sat in the driver's seat. "Does your sister-in-law live anywhere close to the hotel?"

Harrison shook his head. "No idea. I didn't have a

chance to confirm before now. I'll see once we're checked in."

"Did you tell her you were coming?"

Harrison shook his head.

Logan glanced at him and said, "Some history or problem there?"

"Not sure," Harrison said easily. "My parents have been asking me to check on her."

"What's the story?"

"My brother was killed in a car accident, and his wife lost the baby she was carrying shortly thereafter. Haven't heard a whole lot from her since."

"Wow, okay. That's a lot of really depressing news all at the same time." Logan thought about it and said, "She's probably moved on completely. I'm sorry about your brother and your niece or nephew."

"Tough times for all of us back then." Harrison glanced at him. "Have you contacted your friends?"

"Not yet." Logan winced. "I haven't stayed in touch, so not sure who's even still around. But for some reason, I really wanted to come to Boston."

"Were you close with any of them?"

"No. Not really. Just friends with the group. Still it might be nice to touch base. If it doesn't work out, that's fine too."

At the hotel, they checked into their room. Harrison sat down to figure out where his sister-in-law lived, comparing her location to the hotel's and to the addresses Levi had given them to check out.

Logan walked out onto the balcony to make his calls. Half an hour later he was no further ahead. One of the guys had laughed and said he wasn't even in Boston anymore.

Another got back to Logan and said he was on vacation in Hawaii. When Logan called Kandy, it never went through. Logan shrugged. That's what he got for not making plans ahead of time.

He went inside to see if Harrison had any more luck and found he'd already mapped out the known addresses for a quick drive-by. He'd also talked to his sister-in-law, who wasn't interested in a reunion. She'd moved on. Apparently that worked for Harrison too.

Logan checked his watch. "We have time this afternoon to check out a couple of those addresses."

They were back outside in the vehicle, the GPS on the rental already programmed. They hit the first one in a relatively wealthy section full of brownstone townhouses. Lots of parks, nice family area. They didn't drive around; instead they stopped and parked. They walked several blocks to a park and sat, studying the layout and address in question. The numbers on the house were clearly visible. It was a quiet, unassuming area—no sign of anybody coming or going. The curtains on the upstairs bedroom windows were closed. Logan studied the residence for a long moment and said, "I didn't get any hits on this. What about you?"

Harrison shrugged. "It looks deserted to me. I'm not getting any vibe off it at all."

They returned to the car to drive to the next address. On the way, Logan said, "Did you hear us? Talking about vibes and hits? How different is that from Terk and his warnings?"

"I'd like to think my vibes are more from years of experience looking for trouble."

"Absolutely. That's how I feel. But maybe that's what Terk feels too. Maybe he has a more developed instinct than we do. Perhaps that's what his insight is."

Harrison nodded. "Whatever it is, I'm not too bothered. If he doesn't start wearing a great big turban and carrying a glass ball, I'm good."

"I've never met the guy. Have you?"

Harrison laughed. "I haven't."

"Alfred appears to take Terk quite seriously too. He knew of him from the military as well."

Harrison turned to him in surprise. "Alfred?"

Logan nodded.

"Wow."

The second address appeared to be an apartment. They parked, then got out and walked the block, checking to see what the area was like. It looked middle-class family. No security system was on the main entrance, but as they stepped up, somebody unlocked the door and let them in. They headed toward the correct apartment, taking the stairs to the fourth floor.

They stepped into the hallway, found the apartment number but of course, saw no name or identification.

As they walked toward the elevator, one of the neighbors came out, and Logan spoke with her.

She smiled. "I've heard women at various times, but I don't know them and haven't seen one for months." With a shrug, she added, "I did hear some banging and noises the other day, but that's all. It's been damn quiet since." She beamed at them as she pushed a button to close the elevator door. "I did hear him yell at a woman this morning though, so maybe he has a new girlfriend."

As the door closed, Harrison asked, "I don't suppose you got anybody's name, did you?"

"Oh my, yes. This morning he called her Alina. I remember thinking that was such a pretty name." Then the double doors closed in front of her.

"Alina?" Logan asked as he glanced toward the apartment, his vibe triggering a strange feeling. "I'm definitely getting a hit on this place."

He walked to the apartment and pressed his ear against the door. No sign of anything. He gave a hard knock. Nobody answered. Harrison joined him as he knocked a second time. This time he thought he heard crying. "We have to check this out."

"We're going in?"

Logan already had his tools. The door opened in seconds. With a quick glance to make sure they were alone, he slipped inside with Harrison on his heels. This was not legal, and Levi certainly wouldn't sanction it, but they had to get in. Sometimes one had to follow instinct, and right now, Logan's was screaming at him.

Chapter 2

ALINA DROPPED HER head on the pillow, crying as that movement stretched her shoulders and twisted her neck, worsening the pain. How the hell had she gotten into this mess? And how would she get out? Colin was gone for a few hours—or so he said. It was the first time he'd left her alone. Therefore, her only window of opportunity. But that didn't help if she had no way to escape. She'd been here for two days. Two long days—as best she could remember. But the fate awaiting her was worse. The last thing she wanted was to be raped, but according to him, it was all she'd ever know after this. She shifted on the bed and once again tried to release the bindings on her wrists. Both were tied to one corner of the bed. Her ankles to the other bedpost kitty-corner.

She'd pleaded with him to not tie her up, but he hadn't listened. And she knew the longer she lay here, the more numb her body would get. That would almost be a gift right now. She had to get the hell out. But how?

Then she heard the door pop open. She froze. Colin hadn't been gone long enough yet. And if he was already back, she was out of time. And then what the hell would she do? She'd lost her one chance at freedom.

With hot tears in her eyes she couldn't wipe free, she listened for his footsteps. But she could not still the panic inside. She'd been in and out of a brain fog since she'd made the mistake of having coffee with him at the hospital cafeteria and found herself in deep trouble.

When she heard more footsteps than before, she froze in fear. Was the place being broken into or was it Colin? If it was him, and she cried out for help, he'd beat the crap out of her, like he had last time.

But what would an intruder do? Release her or laugh at her or ... something much worse?

And then she remembered Colin's threat. He had guys looking for women. White women. Blondes. And they would pay a premium price. She shuddered. She couldn't imagine that any robber breaking into this apartment would be worse than Colin's buddies.

Her voice hoarse, she called out, "Help. Please help."

More silence.

And she waited. Please let that not be Colin sneaking in to test her. A man popped his face around the doorway. She heard his startled exclamation, followed by the appearance of a second man.

She didn't recognize either of them. She stared at both terrified and yet filled with hope. "Please untie me," she begged. "Help me get away before he gets back."

The men rushed to her side, one going to her hands, the other moving toward her feet. The man at her hands studied her face as he worked to untie her bindings and asked, "Who the hell did this to you?"

She stared up at him. "Colin Fisher. He's the man who tied me up."

He froze, then went back to her bindings.

She knew her mind was fuzzy, but it didn't make any sense that they had broken into an apartment and didn't know whose it was. Unless they were casing the joint. But then why stick around now? "Did you not know who lived here when you broke in?"

The first man shot her a hard glance and asked, "How do you know we broke in?"

She was about to answer, but her hands were freed then, and her arms fell to the bed. She cried out as pain screamed up them to her shoulders. The man grabbed her arms and gave them a good shake before massaging them.

"Take it easy," he said. "If your arms have been like this for a long time, it'll hurt like crazy to move them."

She gasped, unable to stop the tears in her eyes. "You're not kidding. I've been like this since this morning when he left. But he's kept me tied up off and on for two days now."

"Any idea where he's gone?"

"To meet his friends. The ones he keeps threatening me with."

The second man at her feet finally released her legs. He worked the bottom of her calves and the soles of her feet and ankles, massaging them as he slowly moved her legs up and down, bending her knees.

The pain coursing through her made it impossible to speak. When she could, she said, "Colin told me he knew men who would buy women like me."

"Like you?" the man nearest her asked.

She shot him a confused look. "I presumed he meant any women that crossed him because I wasn't giving him what he wanted."

The man stopped and stared down at her. "Did he rape you?"

She shook her head. "I've been out of it most of the time. I don't think so, but he gave me an ultimatum. He said if I didn't agree to submit, he'd sell me to these men."

"Still rape. No matter which way you cut it." He bent down and picked her up in his arms, carrying her out to the living room. "And he likely planned to sell you regardless. He would get something for himself and terrorize you even more."

She didn't know if she should clutch him or try to run away. Once he placed her in a chair, she realized how rubbery her legs were, as well as her arms.

He continued massaging her legs and feet, getting the blood moving once again.

She gave him a wobbly smile and said, "Thank you." She glanced at the door. "We really need to get the hell out of here."

"Tell us more about Colin," the first man said. "We can't let him do this again."

She shook her head, as if clearing it. "I'm a nurse. He said he worked part-time as an orderly. He kept asking me out, and I refused. After that it was just a nightmare, as if I was already his girlfriend and just being difficult. He kept stalking me. He finally caught me in the cafeteria, and I sat and had coffee with him."

"Did you call the police, report the stalking?" the second man asked.

She nodded and wrapped her arms around her shoulders. "I was hoping he'd stop then. But I don't remember anything after having coffee." She stared at the strangers. "Who the hell are you guys anyway? Not that I'm not grateful. I really want to get out of here." She glanced around, not even giving them a chance to answer and asked, "Is my purse here?"

"I'll look," the second man said.

The first man stopped massaging and gently put her foot on the floor.

"Thank you. I'm Alina Chambers," she whispered. "Who are you?"

"I'm Logan, and my buddy is Harrison. We work for a Texas private security company." He gave her a lopsided grin. "You're lucky we showed up to check out this apartment for a potential problem."

She stared at him blankly. "I'm sure this makes sense to you, but it doesn't to me." She pushed her hands down on the chair and struggled to her feet. "I have to leave before he gets back. Where are my shoes and purse? I can call the cops, but I'm afraid he'll get bail and be out on the streets after me in no time."

She took a couple steps and had to hang on to the wall for support. "How can I be so weak?"

"Did he give you any drugs?" Logan asked at her side, putting an arm around her shoulders to support her. He helped her to the front door and pointed to a set of women's boots on the floor. "Those yours?"

"Yes," she cried gratefully. He bent down and lifted first one foot and then the other. Using his back for support, she stepped into her boots.

She felt better already. What was it about having boots that gave her a little more security and self-confidence?

"Logan?" Harrison's voice came from the other room. "You need to see what I found."

Logan straightened and patted her on the shoulder. "Stay here at the door. Let me see what he discovered."

She leaned against the wall next to the front door, wondering if she could go outside. Surely it was a whole lot safer than being inside. But she really wanted her purse. She waited a long moment, then struggled toward where the men had disappeared. She found them in the kitchen.

At her arrival, Logan turned and asked, "Are any of these yours?" On the table was an assortment of purses.

Shocked, she could feel herself swaying. She clung to the counter as she studied the neat rows and counted fifteen of them. Her bones turned to rubber, and all the heat drained from her body. She whispered, "How many women has he done this to?" She took a deep breath and nodded to the purse on the far end. Even her joy at seeing it didn't begin to wipe out the enormity of what they'd found. "The burgundy leather one at the far end looks like mine."

Logan picked it up, opened it and gave it to her. "Your wallet is still in there."

"Where did you find these?" she cried out, going through her wallet and purse in relief.

Harrison pointed to cupboard above the fridge. "They were up there in a box."

Leaning against the kitchen counter, she quickly went through hers. "My apartment and car keys, wallet, money, and even credit cards are all still in here." She reached up a hand to wipe her forehead. "That's a relief. What do we do about all those?" She pointed to the remaining ones. "If a woman has gone missing for every purse here ..."

The two men exchanged hard glances.

"We have to call the police," she said reluctantly. "He has to be stopped."

Logan glanced at her and asked, "Do you live in Boston?"

Her eyes grew wild. "Boston? I'm in Boston?" She shook her head. "No, I live in Somerville and work at the university hospital there."

"That's, what? A half hour from here?"

She gave a quick nod, then covered her mouth with her hands.

Logan lifted her arm.

She glanced down to see the swelling at the top of her shoulder. "So he did drug me." She watched his face as he nodded.

"Looks like it. And it doesn't look like your system appreciated it either." He glanced at Harrison. "She needs a hospital."

"And we should contact Levi."

"Who's Levi?" Alina asked, now suspicious about any newcomers in her life.

"Our boss," Logan told her.

"They were right about the trafficking ring," Harrison said.

"Crap," Alina said. "I thought he was just using that as a threat."

Logan pointed at the line of purses. "I highly doubt this is a purse-snatching problem."

She started to shake, and then tears sprang to her eyes. She turned and leaned on the counter, feeling her breath whooshing out of her body. "Oh, my God! How close did I come to ending up like these poor women?"

"Damn close I'd say." Logan stayed at her side, gently rubbing her shoulders and back. He turned to Harrison. "Want to call Levi from the other room?" He turned to her, bending down to study her face.

She gave him a wan smile and said, "I'm okay. Honest, I'll be fine."

He nodded. "You are now. Do you have any idea how long ago Colin left and when he's supposed to be back?"

"He said a couple hours." She closed her eyes, trying to think. Time seemed so unreal. "I'm not sure how long ago that was. I was lying there, figuring out how to get free. This is the first time he's ever left me alone."

"You sure he didn't touch you?"

She stared at him with tears growing in her eyes. "How am I supposed to know? If he drugged me, how would I even..." And she started to cry.

He turned her into his arms and held her close. "Take it easy. You've been through a huge ordeal, but you're safe now."

She shook her head, her tears dripping onto his shirt, and mumbled, "How can you say that? We're still in this place where I was held captive. You haven't caught the bad guy yet. And I highly doubt you'll do so now. But I can't let him go free."

"You don't have much trust in the legal system, do you?"

She shook her head. "I'm a nurse, and had worked in one of the poorer areas in town. It was incredible the amount of repeat people we saw. Abused women, gang fights, and rape victims." She shook her head. "The world's a mess out there."

For Alina, snuggling in close to the big and strong man at her side for the moment was a heady experience. She slowly wrapped her arms around him and clung.

He held her tighter. "It's going to be okay. Harrison and I won't let anything happen to you."

She lifted her head and stared up at him. He dwarfed her five feet four; she guessed he had to be at least six feet four. She was small-boned and lean, and he was the opposite—an easy 240 pounds. She shook her head.

"Let me take you to the hospital," he said. "Get you

checked over."

"Then I'll be in the system, and that's not a happy place to be."

"*Trust*," he said firmly. "You need to trust."

She gave him a weak smile. "For all I know, you are two of the men Colin was talking about."

Logan shifted and grabbed his wallet from his back pocket. "I can fix that right now. He pulled out his Legendary Security ID for her to see. "I was also in the military for ten years. I'm not into beating, hurting, or trafficking women." He smiled. "And I like teddy bears, birthday cake, and suntanning by the pool."

She blinked. "What does any of that have to do with trafficking?"

"All I'm saying is, I have a much softer side. Just a normal man. I'm not a monster."

She understood. That was exactly what Colin was—a monster. She glanced at the purses. "Why would he keep these? Should I see if I know any of the women he may have taken before me?"

Hope was in his voice when he said, "Actually that's not a bad idea." He led her to the kitchen table and helped her to sit down on one of the chairs. "We'll do this methodically."

He opened the first purse, pulled out a driver's license, took a good look at the name and face, then snapped a picture with his phone, before handing it to her. "Looks like the money is gone and so are the credit cards. Just driver's licenses left inside."

"Laura Resnick," she said out loud. "No, I don't know her." She put the ID into the wallet, back into the purse, closed it and set it off to the side. They went through the others, and she didn't know anybody; neither did he recognize any faces or names. When it came to the last purse, he opened it up and said, "This is Cecily."

"Cecily Turner?" She snatched it out of his hand. "Oh, my God! I know her. She works at the same hospital I do. She worked in the kitchen area. She delivered all the meals to the patients."

He glanced over at her and said, "Two of you from the same hospital?"

She looked up and winced. "Hunting ground?"

"None of the other names mean anything to you from the hospital?"

She shook her head. "No, but that doesn't mean much. Typically hundreds of people staff a hospital. The fact that I even know Cecily is mostly because her name is so unique."

Then Harrison walked into the kitchen and said, "Levi wants confirmation the purses are fifteen separate women. He wants copies of the IDs."

Logan held up his phone and said, "I got photos of all of them. I'll send them right now."

Harrison nodded. "Good. He said to wait to see if this Colin guy returns. If he does, call the cops. And if he doesn't, after a few hours call them anyway."

She listened to the conversation, her gaze going from one to the other.

Harrison explained, "This is only one of five addresses we have for the four men we're tracking. No way to know what else we might find at this point."

"Four men," Alina asked cautiously. "Not even sure I want to know about that. Any chance those are the same ones Colin threatened me with?"

"Do you know their names?"

She shook her head. "He didn't say."

LOGAN STUDIED HER face, still shocked at finding her when they broke into the apartment. He could easily cover his tracks for making the illegal entry as he would tell the police they heard something very suspicious, like her crying for help. No doubt she had been a victim in all this. And she was still damn shaky, but they had to determine what she might know that could be of help, anything she had to offer. He shook his head. "This address is obviously of some importance. Did you hear him mention any names? Addresses? Dates? Anything to help track down these men?"

"No, he hardly spoke." She stared up at him, her light-blue eyes gone dark. "All part of the same trafficking ring." She glanced around and wrapped her arms around herself. "I'm getting a real chill, so please can I leave now?"

"Where would you go?"

"Home," she said.

"How do you expect to get there? I presume your vehicle is still at the hospital as that's the last place you remember."

Harrison spoke up. "I'll see if a missing report has been filed for you."

"I doubt it. I live alone. My rent's paid up, and I was due for four days off anyway." She turned toward them. "I wonder if Colin knew that."

"We have to assume he had inside information, like your schedule."

"In the hospital, lots of people talk," she said.

Logan heard a sound. He put his finger to his lips, motioned to Harrison, who raced quietly to the front door and stepped behind it, in case it was Colin. Logan motioned for Alina to duck behind the end of the counter, giving Colin a second or two before seeing her. Allowing Logan and

Harrison time to nab him.

Alina closed her eyes and held her breath.

Logan stood just inside the bedroom, out of sight.

A key was put into the lock, then the door popped open. "Goddammit," the stranger said. "I know I locked this stupid door." He stepped in and slammed the door hard, glancing at the kitchen and froze when he caught sight of Alina. "Goddamn bitch. How the hell did you get free?"

When he started toward her, Harrison grabbed him from behind, put him in a choke hold and dropped him to his knees.

Logan stepped in front of the man, putting up a barrier between him and Alina, his fist out and ready.

"I got him," Harrison said with a snarl. "A nasty piece of shit, trafficking young women."

Colin glared at Logan, but he deliberately closed his mouth and kept it shut.

Harrison forced Colin to his feet, and Logan grabbed the wire strips from his back pocket, tying Colin's hands together and twisting the wire extra tight. It wouldn't stop him from running away, but it would from getting his hands free. Logan pointed to the purses on the table and said, "Care to explain?"

Colin glared at him, a snarl on his lips, that look in his eye … and the tensing of his neck muscles, like a bulldog ready to attack—only held back against his will.

The man's attitude held something vicious, yet he was an average-looking male with short brown hair and nothing assuming about his features. Logan could have walked past him on the street and would never have known he was anything other than normal. Which was exactly what made him so easy to hide from the authorities. Women wouldn't recognize the monster within. Neither would they remember him when asked.

Harrison dropped him on a kitchen chair where Alina still stood. She gasped and backed away to the other side of the room.

Colin sneered. "Stupid bitch. Do you think this will let you off the hook? Like hell! I already handed over your details. They'll get you whether it's here or in your house."

Logan reached over and grabbed Alina before she went to pieces. He tucked her up close and said, "Don't listen to him. He's just trying to scare you."

She turned terrified eyes to Logan and murmured, "But what if he's right?"

Logan turned to study the man. Harrison fished through Colin's pockets, pulling out his phone and ID.

Colin didn't fight. He sat there nonchalantly, as if he had some sort of a security system, and the men didn't know what surprise he had planned for them.

And shit like that always worried Logan. Because too often these assholes did have tricks up their sleeves. He reached for Colin's cell and checked through the contacts from the recent phone calls. He pulled out his own phone and called Levi.

When Levi answered, Logan said, "We have Colin Fisher here. I got a cell, and a bunch of names and numbers." He ran through the man's contacts. "The last two calls were to a Roma Chandler."

"Okay, I got it. Anything else on the phone?"

"Yes, a bunch of text messages here. One mentions having picked up a new product. I'm scanning through it now." By the time he worked his way through them, Logan wanted to shower. It wasn't just dirty; it was pure nasty. "Levi, we need to find this Chandler asshole. He's after Alina."

Beside him Colin sneered again. "I told her. She's done no matter what you do to me."

Logan exchanged a hard glance with Harrison. Then he asked, "Anything in the wallet?"

Harrison nodded. "Let me talk to Levi."

Logan handed over the phone and stepped closer to Colin in case he tried anything funny. Harrison went over the contents of the guy's wallet with Levi. Logan half listened. It didn't appear to be anything too important—his driver's license and credit cards. If they could trace his activities through the cards, it would give some idea where he'd been and who he was potentially meeting. It all depended on if he paid or if somebody else had.

As he studied Colin, Logan saw a pack of cigarettes in his top pocket. He pulled it out, and Colin laughed.

"You lighting one up for me?"

Logan opened the pack and saw only six inside. He dumped them on the table and checked the box. He'd seen all kinds of stuff hidden inside cigarette packs. But this one appeared to be empty. He tossed it on the table and faced Colin. "You realize the trouble you're in, right?" He could feel Alina hiding behind him, obviously shaking, and with good reason. "You're into raping and drugging women so they can't resist, and then turning them over to your guys to put in the sex trade."

Colin shrugged. "It sure beats wining and dining them and getting dumped all the time."

"Hardly. But whatever excuses work for you."

Colin ignored him and turned to stare at the window.

Harrison came back then. He handed the phone to Logan and said, "Help him stand. I haven't checked all his pockets."

They stood Colin up, first checking the inside of his socks and shoes to make sure. In his back pocket, he had a small notebook. When they pulled that out, Colin's gaze hardened.

Logan smiled. "So this is interesting." He flipped it open and studied it. Names and numbers. "Looks like a bookie list." It wasn't, but he watched for any reaction from Colin.

Then he saw a couple names he recognized. Beside the names, first only, were dollar amounts. When he hit Laura Resnick, the first name Alina had read out loud, $14,000 was written next to it.

"How long ago did you get paid for Laura Resnick?"

Colin slumped in his chair, closed his eyes and pretended to fall asleep.

Harrison stepped in front of Colin, blocking Alina's view, and reached down.

Colin screamed.

Logan worried about Alina's reaction, but no way in hell would he stop Harrison for making this asshole talk.

When Harrison backed away, Colin whimpered like a little girl. "You can't do that," he managed between broken cries. "That's police brutality."

"Oh, we're not the police," Harrison said. "And you're nothing but a trafficker, so you don't deserve any rights. Besides"—he turned to look around at Logan and Alina—"I don't think either of them saw anything."

Alina shook her head. "No, but a second demonstration would be nice to see," she said bitterly. "This asshole needs to pay for what he's done to those women."

Logan grinned at that. "Nothing like a little bit of payback to make a victim feel better."

"So talk, asshole," Harrison snapped. "How many women are still in Boston? Where is the exchange happening and when? If we're lucky, some of them, if not all, might still be on American soil."

"Oh, my God!" Alina stared at him. "Do you think that's possible? Can we find them? Save them?"

Chapter 3

JUST THE THOUGHT of helping the other women made Alina feel so much better. Having seen the purses had been like a death sentence. To think this asshole had been responsible for the torment of so many others... she couldn't bear thinking about it. And she'd been saved by a fluke. Maybe these guys could help the other women. They weren't the police, but were private security—whatever the hell that meant. Yet she knew they'd broken into the apartment and saved her and captured Colin.

As far as she was concerned, these guys were heroes.

"I want to help," she said.

Harrison glanced from her to Colin. "Tell us everything you know about the others in your ring—where they worked, what they did and how they tracked down the women. Where the women came from as well."

"How can finding out where he took them help us?" Alina asked.

Logan wrapped an arm around her and walked her into the next room.

Finding it something she already missed, she wrapped hers around him and snuggled close. "Thank you so much for saving me," she whispered.

"You're welcome," he said. "And any information we can find out about him will lead us to his connections and hopefully to where the women are."

"But you guys have a job to do, don't you? Can you help with this?"

"Yes, we do, and this is it. But we're not officially here. The problem is, once we bring in the police, they will ask us not-so-politely to butt out."

She nodded in understanding. "I get that, but any information we find on our own to hand over to them will still move their case forward, right? We have an obvious time issue here. I don't know when I was supposed to be moved to the other guys, but they are still after me—which is a nightmarish thought." She shook her head and squeezed him tighter. "But what if they had a quota to fill? Maybe they're moving all the women at once?"

With a tilt of Logan's head, he moved them closer to Harrison and Colin.

Harrison exchanged a glance with Logan, then focused on Colin. "Feel like talking now?"

"Fuck you."

Harrison reached forward once more. Before he even made contact, Colin screamed again at the top of his lungs, "Don't hurt me. Don't hurt me."

"Then talk," Harrison said. "I don't give a shit if I have to rip each body part off you one at a time. I've got absolutely no patience with rapists and murderers, or child and women traffickers. You are scum. And once you go to jail, I have inside connections to make sure everybody in that place knows exactly what kind of piece of shit you are. I'll make sure your life is nasty. You'll spend the rest of it on your knees in that prison cell with your ass up in the air. So, talk now or forever hold your peace."

Colin whimpered. "Don't you understand they will kill

me?"

Harrison smiled. "If you make me lay hands on you one more time, I might kill you myself. And, if I don't, I can guarantee one of the guys in the prison will, but only after you've been everybody's little girlfriend for a while."

It wasn't easy for Alina to watch Harrison. On the other hand, if ever a man deserved to be terrorized, it was this one. This was the asshole who had drugged and beaten her and who-knew-how-many other women. She stepped forward and said, "All these purses belong to women. How many more are there?"

He glared at her. "I don't talk to bitches."

Harrison reached forward.

"No!" Colin screamed.

Harrison straightened up, giving Colin a hard look. "Answer the lady."

"I don't know." He shook his head. "I've been doing this for a long time."

"How long?" Alina snapped. "And how many did you kidnap from my hospital alone?"

He glared at her. "It was one of the locations where we found women."

Logan stepped closer, standing on the other side of Alina. "Where are you taking them? Are these women alive?" Logan pointed to the purses lined up. "Have they been taken off American soil?"

He shook his head and said, "The exchange is in two days." He groaned. "Shit. If I say anything more, I'm done."

"You're done anyway," Harrison snapped. "Talk."

"And while you're at it, explain why you have the purses."

Colin glared and pinched his lips together.

Harrison took a step forward.

"Leave me alone," Colin cried out. He glared at Harrison for a long moment, but, as if seeing no weakening in the man before him, his shoulders slumped. "Ah, hell." Colin stared at the men, then shook his head. "I wasn't to keep 'em. They're like my trophies—of what I've done. I could keep the cash but had to hand over the credit cards. I was supposed to dispose of the rest …"

"Well, I'm glad you didn't," Logan said calmly. "That proves your involvement in all these women's disappearances."

"Just these ones," Colin protested. "I didn't have anything to do with the others. I wasn't organizing this. I took orders. Not too many, not too fast. All by the numbers. But I don't know what those are."

The apartment phone rang three times and stopped.

"If you don't let me answer that, there'll be hell to pay," Colin warned, eyeing the phone with fear. "These are not people to mess around with."

Logan and Harrison both shook their heads. At Alina's confused expression, Logan explained, "He'll give away his current situation."

"Someone called this morning," Alina said calmly. "I'm not even sure anybody was at the end of it. It could be a checkup call. Plus, it doesn't make sense to have a landline and cell if only one person lives here."

"That's not true," Colin said. "Lots of people have both."

"The only reason to have both," she snapped, "is if you want certain people to use the landline and others to call the cell."

Logan picked up the house phone, checked the last

number dialed, wrote it down, then walked a few steps away.

She could hear him calling somebody. "If you hadn't wanted anybody to know who you are," she told Colin, "you idiot, you should have one of those ancient rotary dial phones. Not a digital that lets you read the call display."

He glared at her but didn't say anything. Logan walked back a few moments later, putting his phone in his pocket. "Where are the women?"

Colin smiled and said, "You might beat me, but I can't give you information I don't have. I meet somebody in the mall, and that's it. We make the exchanges in the parking lot from my vehicle to theirs. The earlier women are lost. Some of them were taken years ago. I'm not the only collector. It's a cross-country system. I'm just responsible for my corner. Hell, I wasn't going to stay here, but we lost someone a while back and are now trying out a new guy. They said when I run low on prospects, they'd move me to another area."

Harrison snorted. "A mall? Not likely. No way in hell you can get somebody like Alina willingly out of your vehicle, and then into a public parking lot at a mall and not cause havoc. And if she's unconscious, with you carrying her, that's even more trouble."

She thought about that. "He has a really large suitcase in the bedroom," she said quietly. "Any chance he's been using that to transport the women?"

Logan turned to her. "Show me."

She led the way to the bedroom. "I only thought about it now when you were talking about transporting the women. Because Harrison's right. No way would they have gone willingly."

Sure enough, a large wheeled black hardcase piece of luggage sat in the closet. Logan laid it down and quickly flipped it open. He frowned. "Not a whole lot of space in here."

"I could get in there and see if I fit," she offered.

He shook his head. "No, because you'll leave a DNA trace. If he's had women in here, we'll find out another way. The case comes with us." He took some snapshots of it, inside and out.

She stood beside it and said, "If you close it, I can lie on top of it. And scrunch up."

As a rudimentary test, it wasn't a bad idea. He closed it, and she curled up on the top of the hard metal, and she'd fit without too much trouble. He took a few photos with her atop the case. As she got to her feet, she said, "That'll certainly narrow down the women he chooses."

"So he's looking for petite women." Logan nodded to himself and carried the suitcase to the front hall. As they returned to the kitchen, sirens could be heard.

She walked to the window and saw two cop cars and an ambulance pull up outside the apartment. She looked at Logan and Harrison. "Did you guys call them?"

Both shook their heads and joined Alina at the window. Logan lowered his voice and said, "Levi would've." He glanced at Harrison. "We still don't have all the information."

Harrison nodded. "After this," he said, "we'll lose access."

He raced back to Colin. "How many women have been picked up right now?"

Colin shrugged. "Alina was the fourth, moving out in the next two days. I was waiting for instructions." He sneered. "But you won't find them. We couldn't do this since forever without some inside help."

"Cops?"

"You could tell us their names," Alina said quietly. "You'll never be released from jail. Why not take the cops down too?"

Colin turned to look out the window, some of the starch taken out of him. "Two cops. But I don't know who. I never saw met them. That connection is higher than me."

"Not quite," Logan said. "We have his tally book, which I'll finish taking pictures of right now." He stepped into the bedroom, opened the little notebook with the money and first names, then quickly took pictures of everything. "We'll access the apartment building cameras, see if they have underground parking lot with security down there and find out how many times he's taken the suitcase in and out of here."

"What a horrible thought," Alina said.

"Let's go meet the locals," Harrison said, as they all moved into the main room.

She stared at the suitcase near the door. She turned on Colin. "Is that how you got me into the apartment?"

He gave her a flat stare.

"That's what you did, didn't you?" She glared at the suitcase with loathing. "I guess this can already be traced to me," she said to Logan.

Logan nodded. "Most likely. I saw blood inside that will help with IDs as well."

She could feel the color washing out of her face at the sound of that. She turned, knowing time was running out. "Did you kill any of those women?" She shoved her face into his and snapped, "Did you?"

He shook his head. "I didn't kill anyone," he protested. "My boss wanted these women. It was my job to collect them, then move them out."

"What was all that bullshit about wanting something from me first?"

"I'm not allowed to rape you," he said. "Damaged goods aren't worth as much. But if you were willing, then I was allowed."

Her hand went to her mouth. "So those women had sex with you, thinking it might get them out of here and that you might treat them better? Instead, you used them and then handed them over, didn't you?"

But he dropped his gaze to the floor.

At the pounding on the front door, Harrison opened it, and the police flooded inside. Logan, Harrison, and Alina explained what was going on. It didn't take the police long to grasp who was in charge and who was the criminal.

When Logan turned and said, "We found Alina tied up in the bedroom," all attention turned to her.

She tried to smile but was suddenly intimidated by that many men crowding around her. She wrapped her arms tight against her chest and said, "I'm okay. Outside of the fact he tied me up for a couple days and beat me up as much as he wanted to, I don't think I have any broken bones or anything. I don't need medical attention."

"That's not quite true," Logan said. "She was drugged, and we don't know what she's been given, but her arm is quite puffy and raw." He lifted her T-shirt sleeve so the police could see her arm.

The paramedics out in the hallway moved inside. She was led to the living room where she was given a quick once-over.

"I still think you should go to the hospital," one of the paramedics said. "This arm doesn't look very happy at all."

"It's been like that for a couple days," she confessed. "It's getting better."

"And yet you noticed it with all the other stuff going on," Logan pointed out.

They looked at the lacerations on her ankles and wrists, and the EMT said, "You should go in so we can take photographs to document all this too."

She bit her bottom lip, completely loathing to do so. Yet she was a nurse, and she had no reason not to trust the hospital. But she didn't know these men, and right now going with anybody anywhere was not a good idea.

Logan stepped in front of her. "Go with them. It's important they get whatever trace evidence they can from your body, and you should have a rape kit done. You can't trust this asshole to say he didn't touch you. You were drugged and unconscious for however long."

She stared at him, fear in her eyes, and shuddered.

He rubbed his hands along her arms, giving her a little squeeze. "I didn't mean to come across so harsh. But the facts are the facts. Until we know them, we won't have the right answers."

Tears filled her eyes as she stared up at him. She tried to nod, but instead she started to shake.

He glanced at the two paramedics. "Give us a minute."

They backed off, and he wrapped her in his arms and held her close. "I know you're terrified," he whispered against her ears. "But there will be no repeat grabbing and bringing you here."

She drew a deep breath, reminding her how much her body hurt, and with a brave face, she said, "I'll be fine."

With the paramedics at her side and Logan behind her, she let them lead her downstairs, out to the ambulance. She was grateful no stretcher had been brought in. That would be the last thing she wanted, to be strapped down again. She sat inside the ambulance, waited as one of the policemen got in, and then she stared at Logan.

"You contact me and let me know what happens." He pulled out a card and tucked it into her purse, then handed it to her, which she had already forgotten about. She reached for it gratefully. "Your phone is in there too. If you're worried at the hospital, you give me a call."

She clutched the purse against her chest and nodded. The door shut in front of her, and she tried to settle herself, knowing a very unpleasant process would begin soon.

LOGAN HATED TO leave Alina, seeing the lost look on her face. If she'd been happy to go, it would've been a different story. He couldn't imagine a rape kit would be anything other than incredibly violating. But he didn't know what had happened to her while she'd been here. This place would also be gone over with a fine-tooth comb, including the bed. They would have to look for bodily fluids there as well. She was dressed when found, but that didn't mean jack when it came to being violated. He quickly retraced his steps to the apartment. He phoned Levi while in the elevator and asked, "What excuse did you give the police for us entering the apartment?"

Levi said, "You could hear her calling for help."

"Good enough." He hung up and realized it was nothing but the truth. He might not have heard it clearly on a physical level, but his intuition certainly had. He was damn glad he had come anyway. Who knew where the hell Alina would've ended up if they hadn't gone in then?

Organized chaos ensued in the apartment. Colin was led out in handcuffs. Harrison stood off to the side in the hallway outside the apartment. He nodded at Logan when he returned and said, "They want a statement from us, and then we're free to go."

"That's to be expected. Can we do it here or do we have to go to the station?"

One of the detectives said, "We can talk right now if you want. We've already spoken with your boss."

"Good. Thanks."

"He told us everything about why you came here in the first place." The detective pulled a card out of his shirt pocket and handed it them. "I'm James Easterly. If you find out anything new while you're working on your own job that pertains to Alina's situation, I'd appreciate it if you'd call me. Our budget is very tight, and our officers are overworked. I'm not against accepting help if any is coming."

Surprised at the man's attitude but happy to hear it, Logan accepted the card. "In that case, fire away and let's get through this. We have a lot of work still to do on our end." He waited a moment, then added, "By the way, Jackson says 'hi.'"

Easterly gave a start of surprise, then his eyes lit up. "Now that is good news. I'm glad he asked you to come."

It took about an hour to go through the full retelling of information while the detectives taped the entire process. Logan wished he had a copy of it himself. Still, he hadn't lied, and, if Alina was going to be okay now, it was all in the hands of the Boston police.

When they took their leave and were in their rental car, Harrison said, "It's not a good idea to split up or go alone to the other addresses."

Logan gave a laugh. "Isn't that the truth?" He shook his head. "We've done a lot of missions but have never come across something like this. Our focus now needs to be finding the other three women before they are moved out of the country."

The police still hung around, standing outside the apartment with Colin beside them.

A sharp noise echoed as they watched a red streak cross Colin's head as he collapsed to the city street.

"Oh, shit." Logan unbuckled his seat belt, opened the vehicle door and bolted toward where the circle of men had been. They were scattered at this point, squatting on the ground, weapons out. Logan kept behind the police vehicles until he got to the side. They all waited. But no second shot came. The gunman had done exactly what he had intended to do—and had left.

Chapter 4

ALINA WAS GIVEN a small hospital room where she waited until somebody could see her. When the nurse arrived, she said, "We're waiting on the detective to come and take photographs of the evidence. Please strip down and put on this hospital gown."

And then it started. How horrible to go through something like this to find out if she'd been molested while she'd been unconscious. Did she really want to know? Then she decided she did. Ignorance was bliss in a lot of ways, but it would forever haunt her to wonder *what if.*

She stripped down to her skin, folded her clothes, setting them on the side of the small bed, and put on her hospital gown. Chilled, she sat up in the bed and pulled the blankets over her. Seeing herself naked had been an eye-opener.

She was scratched, with bruises all over her body; and her hands, wrists, and ankles were chafed as well as sore, bloody, and scarred—already turning colors from being restrained. She didn't even know how long she had been out.

It seemed like forever before a female detective came in. She had a gentle smile when she explained she would take photographs. She wasn't the one administering the rape kit—that would be a nurse or doctor—but Alina had to lie still while her injuries were photographed. And that was when she realized there were more than she even knew.

Including bruises around her neck.

When she was asked to roll over to show her back, Alina asked the woman, "Does it look that bad?"

"It's bad, but I've seen a lot worse," the policewoman said quietly. "Let's hope he didn't rape you at the same time." When she was done, she left her card. "If you ever need anything, call me."

Even if it was a platitude, it was still nice to hear. After this had happened, it certainly made her reassess how she felt about human nature.

Then the nurse came in with a package. She calmly explained it was a rape kit. And, although the process might be uncomfortable, it was necessary. It would be done as fast as possible. As a nurse, Alina had seen the kits but had never administered one.

She'd gone to her doctor for her regular yearly checkups, so the internal exam was something she was accustomed to. When it was over, she lay there for a long moment and asked, "Can I leave now?"

The nurse looked at her in surprise. "The doctor hasn't seen you yet."

"Oh," she said. For all she knew it could be another several hours. "How long until I get the results on the rape kit?"

"A day or two if I can get a rush on it. Otherwise it could take weeks."

While she lay there, she considered how the hell she was supposed to get home, wondering if her vehicle had been towed or if it was still at work. She also should contact her supervisor. She wasn't sure when they expected her again because she didn't know what day it was. Her memory seemed to be quite trashed. She pulled out her phone and called her supervisor. When Selena answered, Alina explained what happened. Between the woman's cries of distress, Alina got the answers she needed. But she wasn't allowed to return to work.

"No, no, no."

In general, Selena was fair but could be a bit of a hard ass. But right now, she was all soft.

"You should take a few days off. I also don't know where your vehicle might be. I'll call security and see if it's still in the parking lot." A pause followed while she scratched out notes. After noting Alina's license plate, Selena said, "I'll call you right back. Are you sure you will be okay?"

"I'll be fine. I'm in the hospital right now, waiting for the doctor to see me."

"I've got you down for four days off, starting today. Call me if you need longer."

Then she hung up. "Well, four days off right now would be nice," she whispered to the empty room. But this wasn't going to be a vacation, so she'd rather be working.

Selena phoned a few moments later. "I've given your license plate number to security. They're looking for your vehicle. Please take care of yourself." She hung up.

While Alina waited for security to call her back, the doctor walked in. He took one look at her and said, "I hear you've been through an ordeal, young lady."

Something about the father figure and his gentle tone brought tears to her eyes.

He reached down and gently patted her on the hand. "You're going to feel this way for quite a while. You should take it easy and give yourself some time. Getting over shock and trauma is hard. There is no real way to make it easier on yourself. But you have to do it if you want to feel safe and secure again."

She stared up at him. "How does one do that? And, when I do feel better, I'll return to work—where I was kidnapped. I don't even remember the hours before it happened. I woke, tied up in a strange apartment."

He nodded. "Some people are never able to really relax in the same environment again. If that's where you were taken from, that makes a lot of sense. However, since you were kidnapped from work, it would help if you could piece together those hours before your kidnapping." He shook his head. "The trauma will often cause short-term memory lapse, but those memories will return. Do you have somebody you can stay with?"

She shook her head. "No, not really."

"It would be good for you if you weren't alone. Particularly in the beginning. You can expect nightmares and a general sense of not feeling safe."

She nodded, but she had no idea who she should call. It wasn't like she had a lot of friends in her life. Mostly coworkers. She didn't have a boyfriend, hadn't for a long time. And, although she wanted to go home, she wasn't looking forward to being alone there either. He was right; it would take time.

He gave her a thorough physical exam and said, "I'll have some blood tests run to see what drug they gave you." He looked at the injection site. "If you don't have any other symptoms, we are probably dealing with an allergic reaction here. I'll get the nurse to give it a good cleaning, as well as your wrists and any other lacerations and put ointment on them." He wrote his notes on his tablet and added, "After that you should be good to go."

As he turned to walk away, he stopped and looked at her. "Do you have any way to get home?"

She shook her head. "I'm from Somerville. Security at the hospital is checking to see if my car is still there."

He glanced at her and asked, "You work in a hospital?"

She smiled. "I'm a nurse."

He nodded. "Good. Then I don't have to worry about you looking after yourself because you know how important it is." And yet behind his words was a question.

With a nod, she said, "I promise I'll take care of myself."

"Good to hear. You've been given a huge second chance at life. I can't imagine what would have happened if you hadn't been rescued. Talk about having a guardian angel ..."

She smiled. "Yes, he'll always be a hero to me."

Then the doctor was gone, and the nurse returned. And like Alina had done many times herself, the nurse washed her wrists, back, neck, and all her bruises and lacerations. When she was done, she said, "Okay, you can get dressed now." As the nurse walked out, she joked, "And I'd dress fast if I were you, as a man is here to get you, and he's"—her voice dropped to a low whisper—"gorgeous."

Alina's instinctive reaction was fear. "I don't have any-body taking me home." She could feel it trembling right through her. She grabbed her pants and the rest of her clothes, and quickly dressed.

When she put her boots on and straightened, the nurse returned, saying, "He's definitely here to pick you up. He said to tell you his name's Logan."

Instantly the fear inside her drained, and she sank onto the bed. "Oh, my God. He's the man who rescued me."

The nurse leaned closer. "He looks like a hero."

As Alina walked outside to meet Logan, the nurse's words rolled inside her head. She caught sight of him standing there, on the phone, waiting for her, and she realized the nurse had been quite correct about one thing. *Damn, he's gorgeous.* It said much about her life that she hadn't noticed this before. She plastered a smile on her face and strode forward, already feeling like she wasn't quite so alone.

AS LOGAN FINISHED the call to Levi, Alina appeared in front of him. With a big smile on her face.

He grinned at her. How was he supposed to explain that Colin was shot dead in front of a yardful of cops? He decided to put that off for now. Besides, he didn't want her stuck in town when they could drive her home or to her workplace to get her car. Not like they needed anything else on their job list, but maybe they could get a little more information from her.

Harrison had been on the same wavelength. Neither of them wanted to see a woman who'd already been victimized left alone, stuck at the hospital, looking at a half-hour taxi ride to get to her vehicle.

"Hey," he said. "You look great."

She snorted. "Great? I hardly think so. On the other hand, I'm done here, and that makes it a lot easier to face the rest of my day." She took a deep breath and asked, "Any news on the kidnapped women?"

He shook his head, then wrapped an arm around her shoulders and asked, "Are you ready to leave?"

She let her arm drape around his back, as she nodded. "Yes. So the nurse was right? You're here to take me home?"

"Yeah. Harrison and I didn't feel good about leaving you here alone."

She squeezed his waist and gave him a grin. "I don't

know how to thank you," she confessed. "I wasn't looking forward to figuring out how to get home. I could take a cab, but I would worry about sitting in a stranger's vehicle, wondering where the hell he was driving me. I don't know this area well …" She shook her head. "This is much nicer. I really appreciate it."

He gave her a gentle hug. "Come on then. Harrison's waiting outside." He glanced at the cuts and bruises on her face and neck. "Do you need a prescription filled?"

"No, I don't think so. He didn't give me one, and the nurse said I could go."

He gave a chuckle. "Meaning you think you can take care of yourself after this?"

"If it wasn't for the rape kit, I probably wouldn't have come at all," she admitted. "But it was a good idea to run some blood tests to see what injection he gave me."

The double doors opened in front of them, and they took two steps outside. She stopped and lifted her nose to smell the air. It was cloudy and smelled like rain was due any moment.

"Remember to enjoy every day after this. Nothing like surviving a horrible event to make you realize how good some things are in your world."

He led her toward Harrison, leaning against the car waiting for them. She smiled and let her arm drop from Logan to reach up and hug Harrison.

He gave her a gentle hug in return and said, "Glad to see you looking so good. Let's get you home." He opened the back door and waited until she slipped inside. He closed it and asked Logan, "You want to drive, or you want me to?"

"I'll drive," Logan said. He'd do better with something to keep his mind occupied instead of the warm feeling of having Alina in his arms. He wasn't sure what to think about her hugging Harrison too. He was hoping she was leaning more toward him. On the other hand, he wasn't in Boston for very long, and the last thing she needed was a relationship that wasn't going anywhere. Right now, she needed a man who would be around, one she could trust. And even then, it would take her a while to get to that point.

But she was a sweetheart. And he really admired her gumption. What was not to love about a woman who could stand up after what she'd been through and get feisty with her attacker?

As he got inside the vehicle and turned on the engine, he checked the area—heavy multiple-lane traffic. He turned and asked Alina, "Any idea how to get to where we're going?"

"Not a clue," she said. "I'll give you the address of the hospital where I work. Your GPS can give you the rest."

She quickly rattled off the address, and Harrison punched it into the car's navigation system. Logan followed the directions, getting on the main freeway. "It's not very far away, is it?"

"My apartment is closer than my work," she said. "But my vehicle should still be in the hospital parking lot. I'm waiting on the security guard to call me when he finds it."

"Smart to have somebody check that it's still there."

"I spoke to my supervisor. She gave me four days off to start," she confessed. "But I can't decide if I'd be better at work, where at least I'll have something else to think about, or if I should never go back, because I'll always be looking over my shoulder, terrified of being kidnapped again."

"Two sides of every coin. You must be ready to face people and questions, and anybody who might know anything about this in their prying looks and intrusiveness.

But you also don't want to stay home where your own thoughts are running around in circles."

She settled into the vehicle and said, "True enough." Alina stared out at the traffic.

Logan kept an eye on her, checking the rearview mirror as he followed the directions.

After being quiet for a long time, she said, "You know? It's bad enough this happened, but I almost feel like work will be a bigger issue. Because I can't remember anything outside of having a cup of coffee with Colin in the lunchroom. So …"

Harrison turned to look at her. "He likely drugged your coffee. You probably got up, headed toward your car, and he caught you as the drug took effect."

She frowned. "But how do I return to work knowing I was taken from there?" She shook her head. "I don't know if I'll feel safe at home either, but at least I wasn't kidnapped there."

Logan could understand how confused she felt, but that wouldn't change the fact she had to adjust to both. "Are you independently wealthy?" he asked in a calm voice. "If not, you have to return to work and face that demon."

"I was prepared to," she admitted. "Until I spoke to my supervisor, who told me to take time off. But her words hit me sideways, and I'm not sure I could ever go back. I'm so confused right now." Her voice darkened in pain. "But I am *not* independently wealthy. Although I do have some savings, I don't have enough to retire."

Harrison chuckled at that. "Few of us do. Logan and I work for the same reason."

"And because we love the job," Logan added.

"Have you ever been attacked or kidnapped yourselves?"

"Many times," Logan said quietly. "We can't talk about most of our military years. But now, working for Legendary Security, we continue to do similar kinds of work."

She shook her head and whispered, "I can't imagine."

"It's not something you ever get used to, but it's what we're trained for."

"I'm trained to save lives, to help people. But when I saw Harrison going a few rounds with Colin, ... all I could think about was how I wanted to get my hands on him too."

Bloodthirsty. He really liked that. "It's natural that you'd want some payback. But mostly it's an outpouring of rage because of all the fear he put you through. Given a few days, you will probably be very grateful you didn't follow through on that first urge." He pulled into the hospital parking lot. "What vehicle are we looking for? Did you ever hear from the security guard?"

"Oh, my goodness. I didn't even know we were here already," she cried out.

He watched as she looked around the parking lot and frowned.

"I can't remember where I parked," she said in despair. "How the hell does that work?"

"Short-term memory loss is extremely common with any trauma. It's the body's way of healing without adding more stress to your system."

"You have a designated parking spot here?" Harrison asked.

"That'd be too easy." She ran her fingers over her face and rubbed her eyes. "I'm trying to remember what kind of vehicle it is."

"You had to give something to the security guard to look for," Harrison said.

She brightened. "The license plate," and she quickly spouted it off.

Harrison punched it into the laptop they always carried with them. "Your vehicle is a Volkswagen Beetle. Black."

"Yes, it is," she said warmly. "I remember that now."

Chapter 5

THEY DROVE AROUND the parking lot but there was no sign of her vehicle. Harrison said, "Alina, the keys."

She took them from her purse and handed them to him.

Harrison said to Logan, "Park and we'll walk around to see what we can find with the alarm on her system."

"Good idea." He pulled into a visitor parking spot.

With the three of them looking, they strategically stopped at one corner and started walking with Harrison pressing the button off and on to see if any vehicle alarm shot off. There was nothing in the front of the parking lot, nor on the side. As they went around to the back they found a single black Volkswagen Beetle. Harrison clicked on the button and the lights flashed. As they got close to it, they confirmed the license plate.

Harrison handed the keys back to her and said, "This is yours."

She clapped her hands in delight and raced forward. She quickly unlocked it and looked inside. "It doesn't appear to be damaged in any way."

"Were you expecting it to be?" Logan asked.

She noted the odd tone in his voice, but with her excitement at having found her wheels and part of her life restored, she didn't think anything of it. She popped the trunk and ran around to the back. It was empty. She didn't know if it was supposed to be or not. She turned to the guys. "Thank you so much. Just getting this back is huge for me."

"How far away do you live?"

"Just a few miles. I'll be fine from here."

Logan stepped in front of the vehicle and said, "Have you forgotten something?"

She looked up at him. "What?"

"Remember what Colin said. They already know where you live, and you're going to get picked up regardless."

She grabbed a hold of the open car door and roof of the Volkswagen and stared at him. All the color drained from her face. "Still? I figured once the police arrived it was safe." She looked over at Harrison. They were both shaking their heads.

"There is no way to know," Logan said quietly. "I suggest we check your house and see if anybody's been there."

She stared at him nonplussed. But inside, she was starting to shake. In a bad way. She turned to look at the hospital. "They know where I work. If they know where I live, I'm not safe anywhere."

Logan could see her start to buckle in a faint. He bolted to her side and grabbed her around the waist, tucking her close. When that didn't work and she started to fall, he picked her up and carried her around to the other side of the vehicle.

Logan opened the passenger door and sat her down in the seat. "You're not in any shape to drive," he snapped. "Let me buckle you in. I'll drive and Harrison will follow us. We'll go to your place to make sure it's okay."

"Make sure of what?" she cried softly. "If they haven't been there yet, that doesn't mean they aren't going to be coming in the next hour, or ten. Until this is over there's no way I'm going to be safe. How the hell do I come to terms with that?" In fact, she had no idea if that was even possible.

Logan grabbed the keys from Harrison, got in the car and turned on the engine. "Give us your address."

She rattled it off but stared at him, almost blind. "What's the point of going there? We can lead them right to it."

"And that means you think you're actually being watched right now." He gave her a hard stare. "Are you?"

She stared at him in shock. "Oh, my God! I have no idea." She slid down in her seat until she was hidden beneath the window.

"If you are, it's already too late. Sit back up again properly. We'll drive to your house and check it out." He closed the door, rolled the window down and said to Harrison, "You lead with the GPS."

Harrison nodded, hopped into the car and pulled out of the lot.

She looked over at him. "I could drive."

Logan snorted. "Sweetheart, you're not driving anywhere."

She sagged back gratefully. It was one thing to make the offer, but she'd be much happier not driving. Now if only the men could solve the rest of her problems. She stared out the window, not really seeing the scenery as it passed. They made several turns and she recognized her neighborhood.

"Does this look right?" Logan pointed to the building in front of her.

She nodded. "Yes. That's my place."

He got out of the vehicle, went around to her side, and opened the door. As she stood, she murmured, "I really am feeling okay, you know."

"Good. Glad to hear that. It doesn't change the fact you were held captive for several days. And you've got to be feeling rough. So instead of having to stand on your own two feet, accept the help you have."

He held out his hand. She slipped her much smaller one into it and smiled up at him. "Are you always this protective?"

He looked surprised and then contemplative. "Maybe?"

She chuckled. "Maybe that's why you're so good at it. You didn't do it because you're supposed to." Her smile widened. "But because you're a natural at it."

Together they walked to the front door. Harrison met them at the sidewalk. His gaze drifted from their joined hands to Logan's face. There was a twinkle in his eye when he said, "You're looking much brighter."

She shook her head. "No reason why I shouldn't. I'm away from the hospital."

She led them inside, pulling her apartment keys out. There was a code to get into the building, which she punched in, then headed straight for the elevator. "My place is on the third floor."

They took the elevator up and then made a right turn. "The apartment building is bigger than I thought it would be," Logan said.

Harrison nodded. "And obviously extends quite a bit down the back. We didn't drive that direction."

At her apartment, she hesitantly stuck the key in the lock. Logan stepped forward and moved her back to Harrison. Relieved, she let him open the door.

As she went to follow him, Harrison grabbed her arm and whispered, "Wait."

She saw the hard look on his face and felt her heart drop.

Please let the apartment be empty.

Logan appeared again at the door. "It's all clear."

Her breath let out with a whoosh. "Thank heavens," she murmured. "I don't want to think about being attacked here. Is there no place safe?"

"I doubt it. They paid for you and have all your details. In their minds, it's an easy snatch and grab. He does the work finding the women that fit what they're looking for, grabs you, arranges a meet, does the delivery, and he's free and clear. On their part, he hasn't delivered, so they have the full prerogative to go and collect what is owed."

She shook her head. "You guys live in a dark world."

Logan spun on his heels, looking at her. "And now so do you."

She stared at him, all the color draining from her face. And it hit her that was the reality she was facing. If these men were right, then she was likely to be hunted. She hadn't seen it coming the first time, how the hell was she going to see it a second?

LOGAN DIDN'T WANT her terrified, but he did want her on guard. She couldn't possibly be thinking straight yet. She'd been a captive, freed, checked over, and was now facing the enormity of knowing it wasn't necessarily over.

He needed her to get that message. Loud and clear. And yet at the same time not be paralyzed by it because that was the worst thing any victim could be. He searched the apartment, not liking very much about it. There was just a standard lock on the door he could pop in seconds, and though it was on the third floor, there was a fire escape to the apartment next door, easy enough to climb up, go to the window, which also had no alarm, get in and come around.

The front door alarm was literally no issue. In fact, it could be disabled with a couple snips. This was a mid-level moderate income type of apartment. There were probably a hundred or so people in here, all of them busy, rushing out to their day jobs, not seeing what was really happening in the much wider world around them. He walked through and checked the bedroom window to see it had a screen and was half open. He looked out, thankful to see the three-story drop.

There was only one bedroom, no spare. The living room had a tiny balcony he'd seen earlier. And again, not much of an issue. He could easily put an eight foot plank between apartment balconies and make that crossing without any trouble. People never thought about that, but with time and effort it was damn easy to cross any of these. He turned around, studied the small apartment, glanced up at Harrison and raised an eyebrow.

Harrison shrugged. "Can't say I like it, but what do you want to do about it?"

And there lay the problem. They were here on the job. Already their personal reasons for coming had been tossed out the window. There was nothing like finding a trafficking ring and freeing one woman to completely upturn your plans. And then there were three more addresses to check out. And now just as many women to rescue—and fast.

In a low voice he said, "I can't in good conscience leave her here alone."

Harrison winced. "I hear you, buddy. Well, I hope you have some kind of a good idea because we'll need an explanation for Levi."

Then he considered how Levi really was inside, and how

he felt about Ice. "You know, I think he might actually understand. I'm just not sure how we're supposed to move ahead. We can hardly take her home with us." Even adding that last bit made him grin. "Although I think she'd blend in just fine."

Harrison chuckled. "Then Levi really would have a fit. It's not like we're running a home for the hunted."

"That's not bad. That's not bad at all."

Harrison rolled his eyes and turned, wandering around the small apartment. Alina had gone into the washroom. She should be out any time. They didn't have much chance to discuss this turn of events while she wasn't in the room.

"We should call Levi."

Harrison glanced back at him. "Good idea. You do it."

Logan frowned. "You call him."

Harrison grinned. "No way, man. This is your deal."

"What the hell do you mean by that?" Logan stared at his friend.

Harrison just rolled his eyes again. "Surely you can see."

Logan shook his head. "I don't see dick shit."

"Obviously," Harrison retorted.

The bathroom door opened just then and Alina walked out. She smiled brightly at the two men. "Can I offer you coffee or a bite to eat before you leave?"

Logan studied her, smiled and a gentle voice settled deep inside. A certain truth. "We're not leaving."

Harrison chuckled.

Alina stared at both in shock. "What are you talking about? You have a job to do and I'm certainly not it." She ran her hand up the side of her temple and added, "I can't say I am feeling up to entertaining. I'd like to go to bed," she confessed, her gaze turning toward her bedroom. And that was exactly what she should do. Logan motioned at her to head into her room. "Go to bed. We'll stand guard."

She swayed on her feet, but still, even though her body was demanding down time, her mind was grappling with the idea of sleeping with strangers in the house.

Logan gently took her in his arms, giving her a quick hug. Against her ear, he whispered, "Take the offer, go and sleep. We promise when you wake you'll still be here." She glanced at him gratefully and he realized he'd guessed correctly. He lowered his head, dropped a kiss on her temple and said, "Go."

She shot him a disgruntled look and said, "Who said you could kiss and order me around at the same time."

He knew she didn't mean it quite the way it came out. It was a sign of the fatigue eating at her. He pushed her gently in the direction of the bedroom. "And if you need help getting into bed, let me know."

She shot him a look, walked into her bedroom and slammed the door.

Logan chuckled. "I guess that was a no?" He turned to Harrison and saw a wicked grin on his face.

"And another one has fallen."

Understanding wiped the smile right off Logan's face. "Hell no. I'm being a nice guy."

Harrison arched an eyebrow, but his grin widened. "Nice guy? Hugging and kissing her? Teasing her, flirting with her? Yeah, it's a whole lot more than that."

"Of course I treat her nicely. You forget about any of that *fallen* shit. Damn you for even being at the bloody compound. That attitude has already gotten ingrained in you. Not everybody's going to hook up, you know."

Harrison nodded his head slowly, sagely. "Of course not.

Just the fact that we have already, what? Five couples now?" He shook his head. "Damn good thing I'm doing mostly away jobs. Otherwise the bug might get me too."

"If you think it's biting me, I'll make damn sure it gets you." Logan shook his head. "Stupid conversation. What the hell are we going to do about this place, and do our job from here?"

"I'll get our bags and laptop. The hotel is prepaid, so nothing we can do about that."

"Levi won't give a damn about that minor cost. He'll be more upset if we don't get these addresses checked out." Logan turned to face the bedroom and then Harrison. "How do you feel about checking out some of those addresses alone? I don't think we should leave her. Not only was she hurt, but she could be on somebody's list."

"It's also very late. Chances are we'd be better off starting fresh in the morning anyway." Harrison contemplated the living room. "Well, I'll take the floor. That leaves you with the couch."

Logan studied the minuscule living room. For Harrison to sleep on the floor, they'd have to move the coffee table into the kitchen. And the couch was a love seat, too small to sleep on.

He groaned, glanced around at the rest of the kitchen and hallway. "Guess I'll sleep on the kitchen floor."

Harrison chuckled. "What about food?" He checked his watch. "It's past eleven." He shook his head. "We didn't get dinner, and I doubt she's eaten anything in a long time."

"Pizzas are about the only thing at this hour." Logan walked to the fridge and opened it to find a lot of green vegetables but not much of anything else. "I wonder if she's a vegetarian."

"She probably eats healthy. She's a nurse, remember?"

"Still we have to eat. Let's find anything close by."

Harrison held up his phone. "I've checked. Two pizza joints within a couple miles. I'll call and place an order and then go pick it up. We don't want to have any delivery coming here, bringing attention to the fact she's home."

Logan nodded. "I'll stay and keep watch."

Harrison ordered two full-size pizzas, one with everything and the other just vegetables. Once he left, Logan locked the door behind him. He walked over to the kitchen window and stared down, waiting until Harrison got into the car and drove away.

And that's where he kept watch until he returned twenty minutes later. Logan hadn't seen or heard anything in the meantime.

He let Harrison inside. Placing the pizzas on the table, Logan realized Harrison had brought the laptop up too. Good thing because, right now, they had a lot of research to do.

The two of them sat at the kitchen table and ate.

After a couple pieces, Logan's mind working away on the issues they'd found, he said, "I was going to call Levi but decided it was too late."

"He already knows where we are, so unless we have something new to share, we're better off leaving it until morning."

"Plan of attack for then?"

"We have three addresses left to check out. Three women to find. So not much hope of seeing your friends."

"They weren't available anyway. I'm sorry it didn't work out with your sister-in-law." Logan asked, "Your brother's been gone for years?"

Harrison nodded slowly. "And she didn't have much to do with the family back then. I'm assuming she's moved on with her life. But I know for my parents, she's a piece of their son's life they were hoping to stay connected with."

"Sorry about your brother. That must have been a really tough time for you."

"You don't know the half of it."

Logan raised an eyebrow, studied his friend's face and said, "Tell me."

Harrison gave him a look. "His wife was my fiancée."

Logan froze, his pizza in midair. "Oh, shit." He slowly lowered the food, seeing the pain in his friend's eyes. "So, you lost your fiancée to your brother, and then you lost your brother."

"Not quite that fast, but ... you know. Not much fun for anybody. My parents were pretty upset with her and my brother when they married. I had no choice but to make peace with it. But now ..." He shrugged. "Honestly, I'm happy to walk away from it. I was hoping my parents were equally happy to also. Maybe they'll be able to now."

Logan winced. "That can't be easy."

"No."

"Did you break up with her, or did she do it?"

"Finding her and my brother in bed made it mutual." Harrison leaned back in the chair. "Hence my relationship issues."

Logan stared down at the pizza, hating to think what his friend had gone through. "Did your brother ever say anything to you about it?"

Harrison snorted. "You mean in between me pounding the hell out of him?" He shook his head. "He never did defend himself, never said anything about it. They got

59

married six months later. I showed up for my parents' sake, walked away and never saw them again." He stared off in the distance. "No way to come back from that."

Shit. Logan felt terrible. Not only had his fiancée dumped Harrison to be with his brother, but she had killed the relationship between Harrison and his brother at the same time, and now he had no way to make amends. Not that he had any to make. That was on his brother's head. And his parents had to watch the fallout in horror. "Given all that, I'm surprised they still wanted anything to do with your sister-in-law."

"I don't think they will now. But it's hard to lose a child. I don't blame them for wanting to cling to bits of his life. She was part of the family for years, and they worry about her. She was never terribly friendly." Harrison tossed his last crust into the box. "I'm done. In more ways than one. Not going to be a great night on the floor, but honestly, I'm ready to hit it."

He got up, went to the bathroom, came out, then moved the coffee table out of the way. He grabbed a pillow off the couch, then stretched out on the carpet in the small room.

Logan watched him, almost jealous. Harrison had always been able to sleep anyplace.

Logan was a lot fussier. He didn't mean to be, but it seemed like the minute he lay down on a hard surface, all the pressure points felt wrong, and they hurt. Each shift to get comfortable just added new ones.

The other guys seemed to block it out. Logan felt like such a wuss, so he'd learned to not listen to the pressure points. Then when he woke up the next morning, his body would hurt. Often they were on the move, and he couldn't afford things like that. Still, Harrison was right about one thing they needed to do, and that was to get some sleep. It was necessary, and they would have an early morning.

They also had no guarantee they would sleep tonight. He closed the pizza boxes, placed the leftovers in the fridge, left the garbage on the table and did a quick security check to make sure nobody was out there and that everything was locked up as tight as it could be. Then he went to the bathroom and took a quick wash. On his way to the couch, he heard a sound in the bedroom.

He walked over to crack open her door. He wanted to make sure she was sleeping. Her window was wide open, and a chill was in the air. He closed it about halfway and then turned to check on her. She slept but restlessly, her body twitching. He wasn't sure if she was caught in a nightmare or having a dream.

And suddenly her eyes flew open, and she screamed. He rushed to her side and said, "It's okay, Alina. It's all right. You're just having a dream."

She gripped his fingers and gasped as she caught her breath. "It's Colin," she said. "I saw you in my bedroom and ..." She shook her head. "I wonder how long I'll keep seeing his face."

"Possibly on and off for the rest your life," he said quietly. "I don't mean that to scare you. But our subconscious often has ways of undermining us by bringing up some of our worst fears and nightmares under times of stress."

She let go of his fingers and relaxed onto the bed, pulling up the blankets. "Why did you come in here?"

"I'm heading to bed. I peeked in to check on you, realized the window was wide open and closed it some. And that's when you saw me."

She nodded. "My couch is hardly big enough for you."

He chuckled. "It will be fine. Try to get some sleep. I'll leave the bedroom door open, okay?"

But she had already drifted back to sleep. He watched for a moment and pushed the door wide. When he didn't hear any sound from her, he headed to the couch and reassessed. Maybe it would work. He stretched out. His knees draped over the side of the arm, and his head was kinked up against the other. Floor or couch? What the hell. He was here already. He closed his eyes, determined to make the best of it, and finally drifted off.

Chapter 6

THE NEXT MORNING Alina lay in bed for a long time, acclimating to the change in her reality. She was home, no longer tied up, and in her own bed, alone. The last part she would do differently. Like inviting Logan maybe. But it was too early for that. Besides, he wasn't sticking around.

Hearing sounds from her living room, she froze and then recognized Logan's voice. How comfortable she felt around him and Harrison. Maybe because she knew those men weren't Colin.

She slowly got out of bed, walked to the kitchen in her pajamas and found they'd made coffee and were sitting at the kitchen table, eating pizza. "For breakfast?"

Logan bounced to his feet, his arms outstretched.

Like a homing pigeon, she snuggled right into his hug. It had certainly taken away a lot of the awkwardness, worrying about how she would react to another man after Colin. She stepped back and smiled into his worried face. "I'm fine."

But he wasn't content with her words. He studied her face, then how she moved.

She shook her head and laughed. "Don't fuss," she teased. "Honest, I'm fine."

He nodded, motioning at the pizza. "We ordered some last night. Harrison went and picked it up, and this is our breakfast." He gave her a lopsided grin. "I'm sure it's not your definition of healthy, but we were hungry."

She smiled at Harrison as he munched through another piece. "Not to mention you're big guys, and I highly doubt a little bit of yogurt and some seeds would do you much good."

Harrison froze, the look in his eyes one of horror.

She laughed. "Like I said ..." She lifted her nose in appreciation. "And you guys are house-trained." She wandered over and poured herself a cup of coffee. "I'm going to take a shower. Seems like I haven't been clean for days." With that reminder, she took her coffee, headed to her bedroom, grabbed some clean clothes and went into the bathroom.

Her coffee was too hot to drink now, but by the time she was done, it should be about right.

When she stepped under the hot water, she held in her cry. Not only did it sting, but it was in places she hadn't been aware she'd been hurt. When she turned her back to the hot water, she realized why they'd taken so many pictures at the hospital. She had no idea what Colin had done to her. But she hurt everywhere. It was mind-boggling how lifting an arm that had been tied and held in an awkward position made every muscle ache. She knew it would ease up. But for the next few days, she'd be lucky if she didn't need muscle relaxants on a continuous basis.

She stood, letting the heat flow over her body. That little bit should help make her joints move easier. When she was done, she stepped out, cautiously dried off and carefully got dressed. She took several sips of coffee before realizing it didn't taste right. She picked up her toothbrush and toothpaste and brushed her teeth. When she was done, she tried the coffee again and smiled. "That's much better."

She hung up her wet towels and grabbed her pajamas. In

her bedroom, she put away her clothes and made up the bed.

When she headed to the kitchen, she found three pieces of pizza left on the plate. She laughed. "Are you trying to be polite, or are you really full?"

Logan grinned. "We are your guests. It would be very unkind of us to eat all the pizza without offering you some."

She studied it and realized how hungry she really was. "I don't remember him feeding me. My stomach is pretty touchy right now."

"Probably the drugs," Harrison said. "I hope you get the results from that soon."

"I hope the police follow up in some way," she said. "But honestly, I have no idea what their procedure is. I've never been kidnapped before."

She sat down to the pizza. It was so good, she had a second slice, and by the end of that, she was done. Logan looked at her, and she shoved the plate toward him. "Finish it." She watched in fascination as it disappeared in about four bites.

"How can you possibly eat such a large mouthful at one time?"

"Lots of practice." Logan's face was deadpan as he delivered the line.

She smiled. "Glad to see you guys have a sense of humor, considering the work you do."

She glanced around her small apartment. "And it's nice to know we had a solid night's sleep. I didn't wake up until the sun was up." She cast a curious glance at the men and asked, "I presume there were no intruders?"

Logan shook his head. "A quiet night."

She nodded. "You guys can go. I should be safe here."

Harrison snorted. "What universe do you live in? Because you were safe for one night doesn't mean you are for the next ones."

She leaned back in her chair and sighed. Once again she looked around her home. "I've only been here for a couple years. It still doesn't seem like I've moved in since I work so many shifts. But it's the only home I have." She opened her arms and waved them around the small space. "It's not like I can just pack up and move."

"And you'd have to do it without anybody knowing, so no moving truck, no assistance and no sign of anybody helping you."

"Like that's going to happen." She gasped. "Do I look like I can lift the couch on my own?" She picked up her coffee mug, taking a sip while she thought about it. "It's not like I can stay with somebody. At least not any more."

The men looked at her in question.

She shook her head. "My best friend moved away a couple months ago. She's the only one I knew well enough to be able to bunk at her place. I came here for work, and she followed within a few months. We often did sleepovers at each other's house if we were drinking and partying. And no, I don't have a boyfriend, nor any close family or friends here. Although I do have some money. I could go to a hotel for a night or two, but that's obviously not a long-term answer."

"That would be someone catching these guys before they come after you."

"I'm all for that," she snapped. "I have to stay here. I don't have anywhere else to go."

LOGAN HAD BEEN afraid of that. He and Harrison had had that discussion this morning. They'd also talked to Levi. She could stay at their hotel, but, like she said, that was a short-term answer. Still, it was something.

"We have a solution for the next couple days," he said quietly. "We have a hotel room that's paid for in Boston. You have days off anyway so you could come and stay with us."

She raised her eyebrows in surprise. "That's very generous of you. But what do I do when you leave?"

"We don't have an answer yet for you. Hopefully the police are on this, and there is a fast resolution. If not, potentially we can arrange for somebody to move your stuff. Help you find another apartment. But we can't stay. We have jobs in Texas."

"Texas? Any chance close to Houston?"

Both men frowned at her. "Yes, why?"

"Because my best friend moved there. She's been telling me to join her because the weather is so much nicer. The hospitals are always hiring." She shook her head and laughed. "But I couldn't see myself making a move like that. I was happy here. I quite liked my job."

Logan took note of her past-tense usage: *was, liked.*

"You might want to give that some further consideration due to the situation you find yourself in now," Harrison said, then nudged Logan.

Logan ignored him. He knew exactly what Harrison was thinking. But no way in hell would Logan bring up the subject about how he'd love to have her living a whole lot closer. He had to stay focused, otherwise his mind tended to wrap around this beautiful woman sitting close enough for him to hug her all over again.

When she'd walked out of the kitchen, rubbing the sleep from her eyes, he'd never seen a sweeter sight. He wanted to bundle her up and take her to bed. Honestly, he hadn't expected to meet anybody like her. And it wasn't like they had a relationship. But if she did move to Texas, they might have a chance.

"The trouble is, I'm not sure I want to get locked away in a hotel room either," she said. "You guys have things to do, so you'll be gone all day."

"True enough, but at least there you'll be safe. And think about it, the police will likely contact you again. And you'll be nice and handy to talk to them if needed."

"That's a good point."

Logan reached over and placed his hand on hers. "Honestly, you don't have much choice."

She stared at him in surprise. "Yes, I do. I can stay here and take my chances."

He sat back, a smile playing around his lips.

She stared at him suspiciously.

Finally, he grinned and said, "You could, if I gave you a choice. But something about having saved your life once makes me feel like I must continue doing so. Which means you are coming to the hotel with us."

She opened her mouth in outrage, then snapped it shut. Her gaze went from Logan to Harrison, who was of zero help to her because he was laughing.

"You guys look good together," he said with a big grin. He stood and grabbed the cardboard boxes from the pizza. "I'll take this down the hall to the garbage chute." He let himself out of the apartment.

Alina turned and blasted Logan. "I can't move into a hotel with you two."

"Why not?"

"Because I have a life."

"I'm trying to keep you safe."

She sat back and winced. Colin's voice echoed through her head. He had said she wouldn't be safe. They had her phone number and address, and they would collect, no matter what. She shook her head in defeat. "I need a few minutes to pack."

"You've got fifteen," he said cheerfully. He stood and moved to the front door to let Harrison in. He took one look at the two of them and said, "Did you settle your differences?"

She sniffed, turned on her heels and walked into the bedroom.

Logan laughed. "Absolutely. She's packing and coming with us."

"Good. Levi called. He wants her with us anyway." In a lower voice, barely above a whisper, he added, "And to keep an eye out in case someone comes after her, whether to kidnap her or to kill us. The cops are working on finding the other women. With Colin dead, there isn't much in the way of leads. But they are dissecting his life to find some. Levi wants them all taken down if we get the chance."

He gave Harrison a hard nod. "I'm on it." He knew he had to watch out; he was getting too involved. This was one of those cases that could go south very fast. He had to make sure he kept his heart safe.

Chapter 7

THEY QUICKLY LOADED her overnight bag into their rented car. Logan drove them all to their Boston hotel.

Once inside, they settled her on a bed. "This is yours for the next couple nights," Logan said as he placed her bag by the window. "We'll share the other."

She glanced from one bed to the other. They were both huge. In theory, they could easily share the bed.

But then so could she.

She turned to face the men. "Now what?"

Logan walked to the door and said, "Now you watch TV or something, and we'll be back in a few hours."

She frowned as they headed out. "Bring lunch then," she called out. She gave him a bright smile, but she didn't feel it. She felt lost already. How very female of her. She sagged on the bed as the door shut behind the men. Damn. She glanced around the room. What the hell was she doing here?

Then the door opened, and Logan stood glaring at her. "I can't leave you here alone." And the wattage in his glare grew stronger.

She raised her eyebrows. "Okay, I'm confused. You just left."

"And I came back." He gave his head a shake. "My mind says you should be safe here, but my instincts say you shouldn't be alone."

She brightened. "Glad to hear that. I was feeling at a loss by myself here."

"Being alone is one thing, but doing so while being hunted is a completely different issue."

She hopped off the bed, grabbed her shoes, slipped them on and picked up a sweater. "So where are we going?"

He still hadn't moved. Now he was positively growling. "That's the problem. We have addresses to check out."

"So, am I in more danger going with you guys?"

"Harrison and I have been standing in the hallway, arguing." He glanced toward the door. "Trying to figure out the best way forward."

"Well, the only way anybody would know I'm here is if they followed us."

"Unless your apartment was bugged."

She stared at him as her jaw dropped. In a strangled voice, she said, "I didn't think about that."

"No, but we did. We didn't have anything with us to check the apartment, and honestly we didn't think they'd be that fast. But we have no way to know for sure."

"But they don't know what hotel we are in, and they don't know what room."

He gave her a lopsided grin. "I know all that. I understand all the reasoning. My mind is completely on board with all the logical answers. However, my instincts can't be ignored."

She considered that for a long moment, thinking of all the times she'd returned to a patient's room because she'd felt like they were either in distress or heading into a major issue she could stave off. She stepped forward and said in a low voice, "I'm prepared to listen to that. I'm okay to sit in the vehicle the whole time."

"You have to do exactly what we tell you when we tell you. No hesitation."

And with that, her eyebrows rose. "I do work in a hospital," she said to make him feel better. "I do follow orders and deal with emergencies."

He studied her carefully.

When he relaxed, she realized she had passed some sort of test. "Good." She led the way to the door. "What route do we take, and when can we have lunch?"

He laughed. "You should have had more than two pieces of pizza for breakfast."

"I've been trying to lose ten pounds," she confessed.

"You've been what?"

At the shock in his tone, she turned to face him. "My last boyfriend said I wasn't slim enough. I guess I hung on to some of that."

With the door locked, they stood in front of the elevator as Logan viciously punched the button to call it. "That's ridiculous," he said. "If you lose any more weight, you'll disappear on us." And then his voice turned crafty as he gave her a sideways glance. "Just think, if you lose it, you could be kidnapped and stuffed into a smaller suitcase."

"That's not funny," she snapped, as they both got on the elevator.

"No, it's not. But now you can think about that if you try to take off more weight. You're perfect as you are, so leave it alone." Logan shook his head. "What is it about women and weight anyway?"

"You don't understand. I like to eat. *I really* like to."

Logan stared at her and shook his head. "The universe is laughing at me right now."

She stared at him in confusion as the elevator landed and

the double doors opened. "Why? Because you don't like to see women eat?" she challenged.

He grabbed her arm, pulled it through his and led her to the vehicle out front. "No," he said with a chuckle. "The exact opposite. I am suddenly surrounded by tiny women who can eat like crazy. I swear they outeat all my male friends."

Harrison twisted around in the driver's seat as they both got in the car. "Hi. Are you okay to come with us today?"

"I was actually quite lost in the room and wondered what the hell I was doing there."

He nodded. "We're still not sure this is the right thing to do, but it seemed wrong to leave you."

"I'm good with that," she said.

They drove away, and she sat in the back with her tablet. She'd be fine to sit here and watch. She was safe; she had the men with her. Although they were strangers in many ways, she knew who they were inside. Heroes.

As she listened, she could hear the men discussing every detail. With the first address up on the GPS, they followed the directions, taking them to an old residential area, with money from the looks of it.

"Wow, look at some of these houses," she whispered. She didn't know if this counted as big money anymore with all the billionaires in the world, but it certainly counted as it in hers.

"They are something." Logan tapped the GPS. "It's the right address." Harrison slowed, and they drove past a big-gated property. It was a majestic brick-and-stone house. A mixed siding that should've been at odds with each other, but somehow it all pulled together into a beautiful facade with even rooftop decks all the way around.

Harrison pulled the vehicle past the house, made a U-turn at the next intersection when traffic allowed and slowly drove past again. "I guess these places have no alleyway?"

She stared at the huge circular driveway in the front yard but also saw an entrance toward the rear. "How do they even get municipal service here? Garbage pickup, all that stuff. Surely that's at the back. I can't imagine anything this gorgeous having anything so disgusting in front," she said with a laugh.

Harrison turned left at the next street and went around the block. "No alleyway but a road." *Interesting.* And because the house appeared to take up the block, it didn't abut another house but a back entrance used for servicing.

At the front, Harrison parked and hopped out. "Back in a moment."

They watched as he strode up to the security gates. Instantly a uniformed guard stepped out to meet him. Harrison spoke with him for a moment, then was ushered toward the car.

"That's what I expected," he said when back inside. "No information and no leeway. Security is tight."

"It's owned by an Italian company. The owner is Dorian Mutually," Logan said.

"I don't know that name." Harrison glanced at Logan. "And this one we'll give the cops to check out. Otherwise, we'll need to make a night trip to check it out."

Alina could see the two men taking notes, texting information back and forth with someone. They must have quite the headquarters they sent details to. It was a fascinating concept to think of the type of work they did.

When they drove past the block and didn't turn around again, she asked, "Aren't you going to check this place out?"

"There is security front and back. We have no reason to approach. But if we wanted to get inside, we would, just not during daylight."

Her eyes widened as she considered them breaking and entering a property like that. But then she remembered them doing the same where she'd been held. "If you had probable cause? Then we can call the cops."

Logan turned and flashed her a smile. "Like we did with you."

"You didn't have that with me." She sank back in her seat. "I just realized how much of a risk you took, breaking and entering into that place, and how damned grateful I am you listened to your instincts."

"In our business instincts are very important," Harrison said quietly. "We don't take anything like that lightly." He pulled out into the main traffic and headed toward an intersection. He took a left onto a main road, and they drove around for another twenty minutes.

She realized they were heading to the next address. "What exactly are you looking for here?"

"Anything and everything." Logan settled back against the seat. "We're after information."

She digested that slowly. "Is that the work you do?"

"Not often," he said cheerfully. "But I'm not against this type."

"And these addresses?"

"Supplied by a street informant. We've been asked to check them out."

"Wow, and you found me at one of them." She stared out the window. "So the big fancy house we just saw would have enough room to house the other women."

"Possibly. I've got an email in to Detective Easterly to

check it out. He has more police resources now that the priorities have changed. We need to find the three women. They can get a warrant to check out this house based on what we have so far."

HARRISON SPOKE UP. "We'll be at the next address in another couple blocks. Look lively, people."

Logan settled back in, understanding exactly what Harrison meant. It had nothing to do with glancing around as much as it did with being alert and listening to his instincts. If they had gotten Colin to talk, they might have had something more to go on. That reminded Logan to check in with the police in the next couple hours. Detective Easterly hadn't been in this morning when Logan had called. And he could use an update on the case.

At this point, they came up to a series of townhouses and a large family-oriented complex of at least eighty units. It was one of those subdivisions where every house was a cookie cutter of the next. About ten were sandwiched together in a single block.

"Looking for number fourteen," he said.

Harrison slowed ever-so-slightly as they drove past the fourth house on the first block. It faced the main street and was scrunched in the middle of several others. The only thing different was the curtains were closed upstairs. He drove to the back, finding more complexes. Finally, he went around to the beginning and entered through the main entranceway. No security gate was here; he drove in and past number fourteen. On the side was a single carport, empty. Harrison pulled into the guest parking space. The guys looked at each other.

"We can take a walk," Harrison said.

From the back Alina said, "Let me go with Logan to make it look like we're a couple thinking about buying, and you sit here."

Logan looked at her. "It's a good idea."

When she stepped from the vehicle, he reached for her hand. When she placed hers in it, they walked together around the complex. Alina talked about the nice playground for children and the common building in the center for birthday parties and meeting rooms.

He looked at the security—or complete lack of it. Although a lot of people and families were here, too much coming and going would be ignored. Unless they found a talkative nosy neighbor who kept watch. Still, number fourteen looked innocuous and innocent. Back at the car Logan asked Harrison, "You want to knock?"

Harrison nodded. He walked straight through the carport to the back door. At the kitchen, he knocked several times.

When he did it again, Logan watched if anybody peered through the windows to see who was at the door. But there was no answer or movement inside. The place appeared to be empty.

Harrison turned to Logan, making a hand motion. Harrison grabbed the knob and turned it. The door opened. Seconds later Harrison grimaced, and he hurriedly closed the door again.

Logan turned to Alina. "I want you to sit in the back of the vehicle and lock the door behind you. Do not get out of the car, and do not come into the condo."

She glanced at him with worry. "What is it? What's wrong? Are the women in there?"

Unable to help himself, he gave her a kiss on the temple. "I'm not sure yet. I have to go look."

He led her to the vehicle and unlocked it. Before she sat, she asked, "Somebody's dead inside that house, aren't they?"

He stared at her in surprise. "I don't know, but from the look on Harrison's face, maybe." He shut the door, heard the lock click and walked over to Harrison.

Harrison was on the phone with Levi. He opened the door again and stepped inside.

Logan followed. The smell of decay was rampant. Not only did it smell of death, but it was one that had been here for a while. Whoever or whatever had died had been so for a couple of days.

They did a quick search of the downstairs—small, cramped rooms, nice enough for maybe two people though not Logan's style at all—but it was empty. They did a quick dash up the stairs, calling out in case anybody was still here. They did a walk-through of the first bedroom and headed to the master. At the door, Logan nudged it open with his boot, just in case. There on the bed lay a dead man.

More to the point, it was one of the four missing human traffickers—Jason Markham. Logan turned to look at Harrison. "And once again things have gone to shit."

Chapter 8

ALINA SAT IN the car, her body twisted so she could look out the rear window. It seemed forever before Logan and Harrison reappeared. She wasn't sure what to make of that. They stood outside, their faces grim, and she knew it was worse than they had expected. She felt sorry for whoever was in the house. Hopefully only one dead body was involved. Still, as a reminder of how grim her own reality was, it was effective.

She didn't know if this was connected with her abduction, but she did know Logan had saved her. She wanted to get out and put her arms around him, as much for her own security as to give him comfort. He was a good man.

Logan walked toward her, his steps measured, quick, and determined. So much power radiated from him right now, but anger was also there, like a red wave washed ahead of him as he strode toward her. Harrison was on the phone. She could imagine the calls that had to be made now. The two men who came to only check out some places found a whole lot more than they were looking for. On the other hand, she couldn't imagine what life would have been like if they hadn't come on this fact-finding mission.

She rolled down the window and looked up at him. He crouched down beside her. She said in a low voice, "It's bad, isn't it?"

He nodded. "It's one of the four human traffickers who disappeared. But no women."

She cupped a hand over her mouth. "Oh, my God!"

"Murdered," he added gently. "This changes things again."

She shook her head. "Does it really? You already knew this was a bad deal when you found me, and this is only the fourth address. You still have one more to check."

He took her hand. "After the ambulance took you to the hospital, a sniper took out Colin on the front yard, standing among all those policemen."

Her mouth trembled, slightly opened.

"So this is now the second murder." He gauged her expression, watching for shock or denial to set in. He patted her hand again. "The police are on the way," he said. "We'll wait here for them. I'll try to keep you out of the report as much as possible."

She frowned at him, her gaze a little distant. "I didn't have anything to do with it. Why would I be in the report?"

He gave her a sideways glance. "You came with us, and we drove here. So I would have to explain why we came here, therefore, anybody with us will be a part of it."

She sagged back and winced. "The last thing I want to do is see any cops right now."

"Understood. Just not an option. However, you didn't go into the house. You haven't seen anything. You don't know anything. You're sticking close to me because I'm the one who rescued you."

She brightened. "Now that much I can do. And you should get a medal for saving me from that asshole, Colin."

She was back to bloodthirsty, so he was glad about that. "Like an Alina medal?"

She wrinkled up her face, then she realized what this would mean. "I guess lunch is delayed?"

He chuckled. "Not so much. Harrison and I will search the house, see if we can find out anything before the police get here. You have to stay here out of sight and don't leave the vehicle. Otherwise, I'll have to explain what you were doing."

"I'm totally fine here." She shook her head. "I'm playing games on my tablet," she confessed. "Anything to pass the time and take my mind off...life."

He leaned in and gave her a hard kiss on the top of her head. "Understood." And he turned and walked away.

She wondered how the hell their relationship had progressed to him feeling comfortable enough to kiss her like that and her to accept it. Not only that, but hate the fact he was walking away without having pulled her into his arms and given her a hug first. She'd started to really crave those. She never thought of herself as much of a hugger. She'd always been more physically distant with people, but with him, all she wanted was to stay in his arms.

She leaned her head back and let her thoughts run free. She was sorry for the murdered man in the house. That added another nasty element to this whole scenario, but he was a trafficker and maybe got his just desserts.

Those missing bad guys had a lot to answer for. She understood the men would turn over every rock to get to the bottom of this mess. She wished now she could get her hands on them. But she wanted to find the missing women first—before it was too late.

But surely the Boston police were already on that aspect. She didn't know how much time had passed before she heard the arrival of the police cruisers without sirens. She sat up straight and watched as three pulled in. One parked beside the car she sat in; another in the carport of the house, and the last behind him. The officers got out and headed to the house.

She hoped Logan and Harrison were aware of the cops' arrival, as they'd been inside for a good twenty minutes. Then both stepped out on the small deck and spoke with the officers. She watched nervously until Logan and Harrison walked toward the car.

"It's all good," Logan said. "We gave the cops our names, numbers, and the boss's contact info, as well as a statement for why we were checking here. And when the door opened, we could smell something wrong inside. We do have a solid history and a background for stuff like this, so when we walked in and took a quick look, it wasn't out of the ordinary."

She leaned forward and said, "Do they still need to talk to you two? Or to me?"

Both men shook their heads, and Logan said, "If they want to, they'll call us."

"And me?"

Harrison chuckled. "Nope, you're off the hook too."

She sat back with relief. "Thank heavens for that. Personally, I've had more than enough of the police in the last day."

On that note, Harrison started the vehicle and slowly drove out of the driveway.

As they left, Alina saw the coroner's vehicle drive in and was reminded that somebody had lost their life here. And, although she might not be delighted to be called to deal with the police, somebody else would love that opportunity, if it meant he was still alive.

"Where to now?" she asked quietly.

Harrison answered, "As much as I would like to finish for the day, we still have one more address to drive by. Then we need to check in with the police."

"Let's do it then," she said. "So far this outing really sucks." She settled into the back seat of the car and watched as the scenery went by. She'd never spent much time in Boston, so the area was new to her.

Once again, they followed the GPS, which took them to a small residential area outside of the main city. Small houses and yards, with playground equipment in the backyards and small children running around.

"This is really a family area, isn't it?"

"Playgrounds everywhere," Logan said.

They made several turns and ended up on a small side street lined with beautiful poplars on both sides. Harrison drove to the second-to-last house on the left and said, "That's it. Number 211."

They looked at the nondescript two-story family home, painted a soft blue with white shutters and a white door. A tricycle was in the front yard. There was no garden but a small picket fence with a gate to keep children inside. Bright cheerful curtains were pulled back at the windows and tied.

She could see no basement. "If there was ever a less likely looking house to find trouble, I'd want to see it."

Logan laughed. "That's almost enough to make me suspicious."

She understood what he meant—almost too much complacency and niceness about it. Then the back door opened, and a woman holding the hand of a toddler and a baby in her arms stepped out onto the porch, then walked down to the grass. She stopped a little bit ahead, easily seen through the wire fence as she let the toddler walk a few steps in the grass before he fell. She laughed, picked him up and stood him on his feet again.

"Still think it's suspicious?" she asked.

"We've seen a lot worse things in our lives," Harrison said. "We never take the surface at face value. But I'm not getting a hit on my instincts on this one at all."

"Neither am I. I think it's exactly what it looks like it is. But it'd be interesting to know who owns it." He bent his head and worked on his laptop.

She figured he got the name, phone number, and probably everything down to the type of food the family ate within minutes.

"The names aren't connected to any of the four that I can see," he said. "The owner is Richard Noble. He and his wife, Tabitha, bought the house three years ago."

They watched as the toddler went up the stairs and back down, joined by the mother with the baby.

"That'll be why they bought the house. Family time. She was probably pregnant with the one and had the second since." Alina hoped to hell they weren't involved. The last thing she wanted to think of was the mother and two kids involved in something as scary as the murder at the last house or human trafficking, like her situation.

Harrison drove around to the front again and parked not too close to the picket fence. He studied the small house, a frown on his face.

Finally Logan asked, "What's bugging you?"

"It's not that house, but the one beside it that has me off."

"Why is that?"

She hadn't even considered that maybe they had a wrong

house number, and they wanted the neighbor instead. But when she saw the curtains twitch in the main living room, and a face look out only to jerk back again, she realized he was completely right. "Did somebody give you the wrong address on purpose?"

"Informants can give you all kinds of shit for numerous reasons," Logan said calmly. "Just like you. It could be simply the fact that somebody knew Colin was up to this or had seen something suspicious." He shook his head. "Unless the intel is three years old, I don't see this house being involved. But the house beside it, yes, it's all too possible."

Harrison looked over at him. "I'll talk to the mother on the other property. Stay here. This is one time when a single male is better than two."

Logan nodded. Together Alina and he watched Harrison exit the car, walk across the road to the front yard and enter the side gate. He called out, and a few moments later the woman appeared around the side of the house with the baby in her arms. Logan and Alina were too far away to hear the conversation, but it lasted several minutes. Apparently, Harrison was getting some information.

When he came back to the car, it was hard to read his face, unlike when Logan had left the condo after finding the dead man. It had been easy to see he was pissed off. She struggled to read Harrison's body language.

When he got back in the car, he said, "The family moved in three years ago. A single male lived there originally. The property was owned by their neighbor, Lingam, and his brother was living in the house."

Silence reigned in the vehicle.

A moment later Harrison added, "She hasn't had anything to do with the neighbor since they moved in. He's a loner, no family, not friendly at all. Keeps a big dog in the backyard most of the time."

"Did you see a dog?" Alina asked.

Logan answered, "I bet if we drive around back now, we'll find the dog is outside. The brother's been watching us from the front window."

"True, but I've seen all kinds of people in my life as a nurse," Alina said. "A lot are plain paranoid and not necessarily for any valid reason."

Logan brought up the information on the neighbor's house. "Lingam. He owned both properties until the one was sold three years ago. He also owns another in the Melville District."

She waited a few minutes for him to come up with more information.

"Doesn't have gainful employment and appears to be forty-four years old. One brother deceased a year ago."

"The trouble is he seems too suspicious," Alina said.

Harrison gave a chuckle. "In our business, everybody seems suspicious, so too suspicious? … Is it really a thing?"

"But you know what I mean. It's almost textbook. Some guy peeking out behind the curtains of the windows, watching everything. Doesn't work, is a hermit."

"I'm not sure he's the bad guy at all," Logan said. "But you've got to consider if he isn't, the way he watches everything going on, he might very well know something."

Logan looked at Harrison. "My turn?"

Harrison nodded.

Logan opened the car door, slammed it closed, then knocked on Alina's window as he walked around the vehicle. She watched him approach the second house, go up to the front door and knock. He waited and waited, and then he knocked again. Finally, the door opened just a hair.

And Logan stepped forward to talk to the occupant.

Alina sat in the car and wondered what the hell he was asking the man?

LOGAN SMILED AT the tall, stocky man and introduced himself, holding out one of his cards. "Good afternoon. Are you John Lingam?" At the man's suspicious nod, Logan added, "We were looking for the previous owner of the neighbor's house. And I understand from her that she bought it from you."

Lingam stared at him with anger and a hint of fear. "Yes, it's mine…was mine," he corrected. "I needed the money, so I sold it off."

Lingam walked with a cane. Maybe that was why he didn't hold a job anymore. And it would make sense as to why he had sold the property.

"What do you want to know about that house?" Lingam stared at him. "I don't know nothing. I mind my own business and stay out of trouble."

"What kind of trouble?" Logan said quietly. "Is there any with that address?"

Lingam stiffened. "Nothing's going on there now. When my brother, Joe, lived there, it was a different story. He was no good. He was supposed to pay rent, but every month I had to fight him to get something. He never understood money, that I still had a mortgage to pay. Every month he gave me a fraction of what he owed me. He was bad news."

"Was?"

Lingam nodded. "Yes, he's dead now."

"How did he die?"

"The way most do in his world." Lingam shook his head. "He ran with some bad people." He stared out at the car. "I don't even know or want to know how bad. But he was shot one day on his front doorstep. I found him."

Logan nodded. "I'm sorry for your loss."

"Don't be. He was an idiot. He got hooked up with all kinds of nasty stuff."

"Drugs?"

Lingam shrugged. "He took several of his own. But I don't think he was dealing. It was way worse than that."

Logan studied him carefully. "Human trafficking by any chance?"

Lingam's face went white, and his gaze darted anywhere but to Logan's. His voice rose. "I don't know anything about that. And I don't want to. If he was involved, then he deserved what he got."

Lingam backed up and tried to shut the door.

Logan didn't argue with him. He said, "We need to find the truth. We're trying to break up a ring. If you have any information that can help these women, I would appreciate it."

Lingam shook his head. "I don't know anything about any women. That's all over with." But he stopped shutting the door. He looked hopeful as if Logan would confirm his words.

"No, it isn't. Not at all. We saved a woman yesterday. But we're missing fourteen right now."

Lingam's eyes opened in horror. "I don't know anything about that."

"Did you ever see any women come through that place?"

Lingam snorted. "You kidding? My brother had women coming and going all the time."

"Did he travel much? Did he have a large suitcase?"

A frown appeared on Lingam's face. "He did buy a really large one, saying he was going to travel. But he never went anywhere. He was too drugged and drunk, lying around the house all the time. He never worked, never did anything. It was hell to get my damn rent money."

"Interesting. I must ask, when he died, did you inherit anything? And if you did, was there any cash?"

Lingam nodded. "That was the weird thing. About sixty thousand dollars was in his account. And I found several more in the house when I cleaned out the place. He lied to me the whole time and refused to pay what he owed, yet he was stacking it up." He shook his head. "That's no way to treat family. And hell I don't even know how he earned that money, and I don't want to. Good riddance to him."

"Do you know any of his friends? Remember any names? Men or women? Anything that would help us? And when he died, what did you do with his belongings? Was he living there alone? Or was there any evidence of someone else there?"

"He was living alone, but, yes, I cleaned out his crap." Lingam nodded. "It's all in the back shed. I don't want any of it. And if he's got anything to do with that human trafficking garbage, I really don't want."

Bingo. Logan gave him a slow smile. "How about I take it all off your hands?"

Lingam looked at him suspiciously. Logan nodded at the card in Lingam's hand. "Our company is working with the Boston Police Department. We'll see if anything in your brother's belongings connects to the current case. I can take it all now." If he had room. He glanced at the rental car and realized it depended on how much there was. "Or I can let the cops know it's here."

Lingam's face shut down. "No cops. I won't talk to them. I don't want to have anything to do with them. If you want it, you can take it now. I sold and got rid of whatever I could. The rest is sitting there. I didn't know what to do with it. Drive around to the back alley. A gate's there. I'll show you, but you have to forget my name. No cops coming around."

"I'll try to keep you out of it," Logan said. "But you understand, they may come back to confirm all the stuff came from you."

Lingam shook his head. "You drive to the side. I'll unlock the gate and show you the boxes. While you load, I'll write you a letter giving you permission. But no cops. I won't even open the door." And at that, he slammed the door in Logan's face.

Still, as far as gaining something valuable from the encounter, this could potentially be huge. He walked back to the vehicle and got in.

After relaying the info to Harrison, they drove around the block, parking behind the house in the alley.

Lingam was waiting for them and had opened the gate. They drove toward the shed. Logan hopped out and swung open the door.

A half-dozen boxes were stacked on one side. "This is all of it?"

Lingam nodded. "That's it. Take it all. Good riddance to him and this crap."

Harrison stepped in and grabbed two boxes, taking them to the car. Logan grabbed the next two. By the time he reached the car, the trunk was open. Then the last two were loaded in beside Alina.

Lingam locked the gate behind them, calling out, "And don't come back."

With letter in hand, signed by John Lingam, they drove away.

Chapter 9

BACK ON THE road again, Alina studied the boxes. They were dusty, old, and she couldn't imagine what was inside. She understood the theory that everything was important and any detail could lead to another, but it was hard to imagine these dirty, busted boxes held anything of value to the case. "Are we going back to the hotel now?"

"Yes." Logan added, "We're about fifteen minutes away."

"Can we pick up some lunch to take back with us first? Or do you want to eat at the hotel?"

"I saw a deli around the corner from the hotel on the same block. How about we try that?"

"It sounds good to me." She settled back, happy to know they hadn't forgotten about food.

At the hotel a few minutes later, the men got out with the boxes and carried them upstairs. Once inside the room, they put everything down on the floor.

"I'll get the food," Harrison said, "and we can go through all this stuff while we eat."

"Okay."

While Harrison was gone, Logan and Alina picked up the first box and opened it, carefully laying the contents across the bed. With the empty box on the floor, Logan went through every item of clothing, checking all pockets to see if anything was in them. He also made note of the sizes for each article.

She felt useless as she watched. "Is there anything I can do?"

He nodded. "Sure. Go through the clothing, check the pockets, see if anything's of interest."

She walked to the far side of the bed and stared at what appeared to be a sack of socks. She was sure it wouldn't have anything of interest. As she looked closer, the socks looked more dirty than clean. She said, "You might want to use a pair of gloves."

He laughed and threw her a pair of gloves from his pocket.

She was surprised, shook her head, and said, "If you'd seen all the things I've seen ..." She put on the gloves and went through all the dirty socks, finding a few pairs of underwear, also not looking extremely clean. "Where do we put the stuff that has nothing in it?"

"Back in the box," he said.

Methodically they went through everything. When they came to the last shirt, he picked it up, checked it out and then put it in the box. Before they could open a second box, a rap was at the door as Harrison called from the outside.

"Logan, my hands are full."

Logan opened the door and let Harrison in. He carried a tray of paper coffee cups and two bags of food.

Placing the food down on the small dresser, he handed out the coffee. Then he opened the bags and handed Alina a large sandwich. They didn't make very much conversation while they ate. She settled back with her coffee as the men rose to start again.

Logan opened the second box, repeating the process with

everything. This box was also full of clothing, including shoes. But nothing else of interest was found.

When they opened the third box and repeated the process, she wondered if this was worth the trouble or if it was all junk.

By the time Harrison opened the fourth box, she could see from his face that he wondered about it too.

He glanced over at Logan and smiled. "We'll have a ton of garbage to get rid of. Hope they have a bin downstairs."

"Me too," Logan said. "I don't know why Lingam didn't do that in the first place."

Alina put down her coffee and said, "Let's do a trip now. It will give us more space."

The men looked at each other, glanced at the two boxes on the floor, and Logan asked, "Do you think you can lift it?"

She laughed as she stood. "Well, only one way to find out." She picked up a box and nodded. "This one's light enough."

Logan picked up the other. "I'll come with you."

She shot him a look. "I am pretty sure it's safe to walk to the garbage area."

He grinned. "But what if it's not?"

Together they walked downstairs and outside to find the dumpsters to get rid of their loads.

Motioning back to the hotel room, he said, "Let's go. After this, I really want a shower."

"Yeah, you and me both," she said. "Sitting in the shed for a year. It's gross."

"More than that, it's probably the way the man lived."

She winced. "That doesn't sound like fun either."

Back in the hotel room they found Harrison had filled

the fourth box back up again. Making a sudden decision, they picked up the two newly searched boxes and headed back out for another trip.

Afterward, Logan grabbed his coffee and sat for a moment. Harrison was laying out everything from the fifth box on the bed.

She really appreciated the methodical way they handled this, although it was frustrating. But still, she likely would've dumped this box upside down, gone through each piece and tossed it as useless.

However, this box appeared to have more knickknacks, books, notebooks, and the odd pair of shoes. She grabbed what looked like a small journal, flipping through it. Every page was blank. She set it off to one side and reached for a stack of papers, pulling it toward her, studying the scribbles on each. She didn't know if the men would throw this out because it was almost impossible to make heads or tails of any of it. She went through a dozen pages and found nothing legible. She placed them with the journal.

Logan was helping Harrison again. They went through the easy stuff—the rest of the shoes, the ties, and towels—until they only had what could be the most interesting of all of it so far. They each reached for a book, carefully checked out the spine, the front and back covers, held the book upside down to see if anything floated out free. One book was a paperback novel. The other a hardback. Neither yielded anything. After close examination, both ended up back in the box. Another twenty minutes, and they finally came to the end of that box's contents. The only thing she'd found were the odd pages with crisscrosses over them, as if they'd been grabbed to jot down notes at odd times, reusing the paper over and over. She held them out. "I don't know if anything is useable in this."

Harrison took the papers from her and sat, slowly studying the notes. He picked up the last pages and handed them to Logan.

Logan snatched them up and said, "Okay."

She lifted her head and studied him. "What?"

He held up the four pages so she could see them. Some of them had stains, like coffee had been sloshed over them. But the last entry was clearly legible, easily recognizable. And why wouldn't it be. It was her name.

LOGAN WATCHED HER face as she read her name on the sheet. Curiosity became horror.

She glanced back at all the stuff on the bed and the boxes on the floor. "He knew me?" She shook her head. "I can tell you that I didn't know him."

"And the question now is, why was your name on a piece of paper in his room a year ago?"

She slumped back in position. "I don't know," she cried in horror. She raised a trembling hand to her temple. "Unless he knows Colin, and they predetermined I was on the list of possible people to get kidnapped." She shuddered. "How horrible is that? To think people were plotting to kidnap me for over a year."

The stack of papers was set off to the side. Harrison, after determining nothing else of value was on the bed, removed everything else, putting it back in the box and opened the last one. And this appeared to be all notes, papers, journals, and books.

Logan said to Alina, "Hopefully this one will yield a little more information."

Once again, with everything spread out on the bed, the three stood and stared at the stack.

She shook her head. "Is this all that remains of a man's life?"

"That and sixty thousand dollars," Logan said. "Let's start with the books, and then we'll go through those loose pages."

Each took a book, and following the same procedure as before, carefully checked for notes or paper stuffed inside, something used as a bookmark that might be of interest, and if it had a jacket flap, anything that might be tucked underneath. Logan picked up a dog-eared journal.

He flipped through several pages; the beginning had been ripped out. Handwriting appeared on the next few pages, but it was very difficult to read. The rest of the book was empty. He checked the very last page, as he had a habit of doing so to write notes sometimes if he had nothing else handy. But it too was empty. He looked at the notes in the front again, not able to determine if they were of value or not. He set it off to one side and reached for another notebook. By the time they'd gone through everything, they found nothing else of value. Now they had all the loose pages they'd set aside.

Harrison picked up a stack. "Looks like a set of accounts scratched onto loose leaf pages but stapled together." He glanced through them. "Not a lot of accounting here. Whether that's him trying to keep a budget for himself or for the kidnapped women, who knows?"

"Do we know when these women were kidnapped?" Alina asked.

"No," Logan said. "So after all that, his address and your name is the connection. I wish we'd found more."

"But that connection is damn strong," she snapped. "I can't say I like seeing my name on any of these sheets."

Harrison was still flipping through lines of accounting entries.

Logan glanced around to see what else there was and found several crumpled-up pages. He opened each and spread them flat on top of the bed. Several contained numbers but had nothing to identify what they were. It looked like somebody doing simple accounting. He set them off to one side and kept going.

At the end of the stack he found another set of stapled sheets. He pulled it up and studied the entries. "And here's a connection to Colin." He tapped the paper and read out loud, "'Colin's asking for more money. He's getting paid enough.' And the word 'enough' has been heavily underlined." He glanced up to see Harrison studying him and said, "Since Joe is in cahoots with Colin, we have to assume he was part of this trafficking ring. Likely one of the minions below the four ringleaders. Joe either was paying Colin or negotiating, so he was caught in the middle between what Colin wanted and what the buyers wanted. Joe was not happy, but he's the one who ends up dead."

"Why would that be?" Alina asked. "It doesn't make any sense."

"It does if Colin cut out the middleman."

Looking ill, Alina sat on the chair, hugging her empty coffee cup. Logan glanced at Harrison and motioned toward her.

Harrison nodded. "Let's finish the rest of this," he said. "We'll have a box of whatever that we'll keep track of. The rest can go."

Although they went through the rest of the pages, they

didn't find anything of value aside from the stack they put aside. This time Harrison grabbed the boxes to toss in the dumpster.

Logan nodded. "I'll take this comforter outside. It's your bed, and we didn't consider all the dirt in those boxes." He rolled up the top cover so the dirt and dust would be contained. Then he stepped outside into the hallway, tossing the comforter into a laundry hamper. He returned and asked, "Do you think you need a cover? I can go find another one."

She looked up at him, confused, then looked at the blankets on the bed. "I'll be fine with what's here, thanks." She smiled. "Truly, I wasn't too impressed with the idea of having all that happening on the bed I was sleeping in."

"We should have had put a protective cover over it first."

He laid all the pages out on the bed again, and with his phone carefully took close-up images of everything. He did the same with the accounting sheets Harrison had. When he was done, he sat and sent the whole lot to Levi, quickly dialing and waiting for him to answer.

"A hell of lot of paperwork you sent us," Levi said.

"Yeah, but it also has Colin's name in there and Alina's."

He heard a low whistle on the other end. "Nice work. That certainly connects the three of them."

"Plus to a couple of the addresses you were sent," he said. "We didn't find anything at the house where we found the dead man." Logan cast a quick glance to Alina, but she didn't appear to be listening. "You have any update from the property?"

"He's one of the four men we were looking for. It's not evident yet why or who he might've known living at the property or even why he was there. The police are on it.

They suspect that the address was a holding property where the kidnapped women were kept and is now too 'hot' to be used again."

"You've told Jackson, I presume?"

"Yes. He's also very interested in the information you found. I'm waiting to hear further instructions from him."

Logan nodded. "Are we to stay here on location?"

"For the moment. I'll call back when I know something more. Still hoping to hear the police have something." Levi hesitated, then asked, "Where's Alina?"

"Right here," Logan said. "I have to admit that my instincts told me not to leave her alone."

"Right," Levi said, concern lacing his tone. "Am I to arrange for a spare bed here for her?"

Logan's eyebrows shot up. He glanced over at Alina. "That would be a long commute. She has a job here and is expected back at work in a couple days."

"Right," Levi said in a brisk tone. "Did you leave anything behind at her apartment?"

"I set the doors to trip so we'd know if anybody went in, and I left a bug in the living room." At that Alina glanced at him. He turned and smiled at her reassuringly. "So far nothing's been triggered on the bug."

"Okay, keep me posted."

Logan hung up, pocketed the phone and turned to face her. "It's the only way we could know if your apartment had been accessed." He crouched down in front of her and grabbed her hand. "Trust us. We know what we're doing and keeping you safe."

Chapter 10

S HE STARED AT him in shock. "It never occurred to me to figure out if somebody had gone into my apartment when I wasn't there," she whispered. She shook her head. "This is a nightmare that just won't end."

He hesitated, glanced over at Harrison, and then back at her.

She leaned forward, her hands gripping his hand. "What?"

"Our time here could be very short," he said. "That was my boss. We're to stay for the moment, but we can't forever. And you may have to face the fact that if this isn't solved, people could still be after you."

She shook her head. "What are you saying? That I should pack up my life and move because of this? How is it I can be safe in another location other than here? Wouldn't they track me?"

"It's possible, but at the same time, if you move out of their reach, it'll cost them that much more to go after you. They might want to cut their losses and walk away. A lot is going on behind the scenes. But at some point, our plug will get pulled, and we'll have to return to Texas."

She gently disentangled her hands and sat back, crossed her arms over her chest and contemplated what she was supposed to do. She didn't have any answers. What kind of a nightmare was this? "What if I took a leave of absence and went for a vacation?" She cast her eyes around the room, as if seeing her apartment, the few belongings she had. "To uproot my life and make a move like this with no job, place to live, or security…" She shook her head. "That's extreme."

"Is it?" Harrison asked. "Consider what the other option is. You stay home. You get relaxed, figure it's all over with and wake again tied up in another bedroom."

Her hand went to her chest at the reminder. She straightened against the chair back, fished her phone out of her pocket, opened her contacts and called Caroline. When the phone was answered, she said, "Caroline, it's Alina."

"Alina!" Her friend, overjoyed to hear from her, bubbled with good news. When she finally calmed down, she asked, "But you called me for a reason, right?"

Alina filled in her friend as much as she could, with an awful unpleasant silence greeting her on the other end. After a quiet pause of her own, Alina said, "The police haven't told me very much at all." She glanced at her watch. "I should've called them earlier to get an update. I don't know if I have to be here for a court case or what, but according to the two guys who rescued me, I'm still in danger."

"Of course, you're still in danger," Caroline cried out. "And that rat who kidnapped you said they would come after you. The chances are very good they will. That's it. You're coming down here."

"What good does that do?" Alina asked wearily. "I'm working and likely would be coming back and forth for the stupid trial."

"Are you kidding? That could be two years from now." Caroline let out a gust of breath. "I've tried to get you to move here anyway, so this is perfect."

Alina sat back, happy to hear her friend's voice, realizing how much she had missed her. "I don't have a job there or a place to live. And I don't have a ton of money. I can't be out of work forever." And yet even she knew those were weak excuses.

"You're just afraid. You're afraid to make the move, like you were when I did. But surely the fear of being taken again must supersede the one of changing jobs and locations. I have a home. You can stay here with me until you're on your feet. And the hospitals here are screaming for nurses. You can move here." Caroline's voice was firm and adamant. "I'll even pay for your plane fare."

"And my furniture? What do I do with that? Am I supposed to sell it?" she asked, her voice rising at the end. "How does that make any sense when I'll need furniture at a new place?"

"It makes more sense than to ship it. All of it was secondhand when we bought it. We can do that all over again here."

"I can't walk away from my apartment, leave everything behind." She made a slow 360 turn, mentally calculating the contents of her place. "I have the couch, tables, and my bed."

"Put an ad for free in the newspaper," her friend suggested. "Everything will go on the first day. I'm not taking no for an answer."

"I'll call you back as soon as I talk to the police." Alina hung up the phone. She stared at Logan blindly. "She's pretty insistent that I move to Houston."

"Maybe the real question you must ask right now," Harrison said, "is why you wouldn't?"

And just like that she saw the enormity of the situation she was in. "I need a few minutes to lie down," she murmured. She sagged on the now-clean bed and curled up with her head on the pillow. She'd been holding on decently for most of the day, pushing back all the memories, all her fears under control because she had these two men standing by her. No way would she be kidnapped with her two body-guards. But they had to leave soon. Then what?

Her eyes were wide open and completely dry, like the issue was too big for tears. The chasm between her old and new life was so vast, so wide and impossible to cross, she had no emotion other than shock.

She recognized his touch instinctively. Logan quickly scooped her up, pulled the blankets back and tucked her under, pulling them close to her shoulders. Harrison was a nice guy, but he was not the touchy-feely person Logan was. That touch wasn't irritable or cranky; it was easy, calming. Logan was holding her hand, giving her a hug, stroking her arms or cheek, or in some other way making contact with her most of the time. It helped her stay grounded in this crazy new reality.

But as she heard the men's voices whispering behind her, it was as if she had been fooling herself all this time.

She couldn't imagine going back to her place now. And if she didn't, where else could she go? She had slept there last night. But she'd had the two men with her. Now she was in their hotel room, strangers but not. She'd never felt safer. Yet it would only last if she was with them, and that wouldn't continue for long. They'd check out as soon they were told to. She didn't know if more was on their itinerary, but they were waiting for orders. They'd been here one night and were supposed to leave the next day. And that meant she had to return to her life. Without them.

When the shaking started, she didn't know how to stop

it. Maybe if she could sleep, it would do her good.

She heard a muffled exclamation before she was suddenly picked up, blankets and all, and tucked up against Logan's chest. The lights were turned down, and she didn't know if it was still daylight. The curtains were closed and she heard Harrison mumble something.

She whispered against Logan's chest, "I'm sorry, so sorry."

He held her close, rubbing her back. "You have nothing to be sorry about," he said quietly. "I've been expecting a reaction like this the whole time. I didn't quite understand how you were so composed."

"I'm not. When I finally realized what I could be facing forever, I understood then how much trouble I could be in."

"Or maybe you were in denial," he said. "It's our instinctive nature to look at things in a positive light."

She nodded her head. She wanted to convince him that she was okay, but the words wouldn't come. Instead, she turned her head into his chest and clung to him. He didn't talk or bother her with questions. He just held her close and rubbed her back. Some of his calm, his compassion, finally slipped into her consciousness, and she could feel the shaking ease. She took several deep breaths, and, lying against his chest, whispered, "Thank you."

"I have hardly done anything," he murmured. "I wish I could've saved you those couple days tied like that, panicking and afraid, worried about where you would end up. I haven't done anything. The problem is, I can't guarantee your safety if you stay here. We could put you in protective custody, but we know all too well how easy it is for somebody to get at the victim if they truly want to." He squeezed her tight against his chest. "I'm not saying that to scare you, but it is the reality. The criminal world has ways, means, and manpower that is almost impossible to beat sometimes."

She lifted her head and looked up at him. "What if you catch the bad guys?"

His gaze was hard and yet soft, determined and yet weary, as if he held too much knowledge of the world.

"We hope we catch all the bad guys, but you know how very slim the chances are, so we must focus on catching all who were after you."

"The only way to do that is... Surely the police will track down all Colin's associates." She was terrified for the fourteen women who had been kidnapped, still caught in that bad situation. "That big house. The expensive one. What are the chances the missing women are in there?"

He shook his said. "We don't know. All I can tell you is we're awaiting orders. We've done what we were supposed to, and I don't know what's coming next."

She glanced around the room. "Harrison left. Did I scare him away?"

"No. He went for a breath of fresh air and to make more phone calls. He'll be back in a little bit. You haven't had much time to yourself. We've needed to stay close to make sure you were okay."

She stared around the small room that had become home so very quickly. "I don't know what to do."

"I'm sorry that picking up stakes and moving is a hard thing for you because it would be so much easier if you disappeared from the grid. The men wouldn't have a clue where you were, and they wouldn't be able to track you."

She glanced at him and asked, "Can you make that happen?"

He looked down at her in surprise. "Make what?"

"Help me disappear. To get away from the city. From my apartment. From that world. Find a job somewhere, somehow." She paused. "It seems so real suddenly. Like the last forty-eight hours wasn't—like I pushed it away into the recesses of my mind—but now I can see how dangerous my situation is. I'm terrified of getting caught again."

"When you say *that world*, you mean your life? Your normal home and job?" Logan kept her tucked close and gently rocked her on the bed. "Well, it's probably a good thing you are more aware now. As to making you disappear..." He leaned back to consider it. "I'm sure we can help you. Not sure of the time frame." He glanced down at her. "How much of this is a passing whim on your part? You could change your mind tomorrow. Or a week from now. If we help you relocate to a new city, and you find a new job, are you going to regret it?"

She pushed herself off his chest and stared at him. "Will I be alive? Will I not be a sex slave or slave labor, or God-knows-what they had in mind for me? I might always wonder if this was a necessary step, but then the nightmares will remind me how bad it was being tied up in that bed, panicking to escape." With that line, she shook her head. "If I have to move, I want to go to Houston. At least that's where Caroline lives. She's been bugging me to move there as it is."

"Oh, I agree. But that's no guarantee they can't track you."

She nodded. "But it's about as good as I can get. It must happen quietly, like you and Harrison said. I don't know how much trouble it would be to change my name. Or if that's even necessary," she confessed. "I make decent money, and I have some saved, but I can't be out of work for six months."

She studied him as she pushed the blankets off her shoulders, realizing she was now sitting in his lap, a new situation for her but she liked it. He looked a little preoccupied, as if contemplating the logistics of making her disappear.

"What about the police?" she asked Logan. "We must tell them something. But it's hard to imagine rings like this operating within the city without some law enforcement knowing."

He tilted his head, his mouth in a grim line.

She hated the thought of the police being involved or at least knowing and turning a blind eye. She wanted to believe they were honest and doing the most beneficial things they could for the citizens of the city.

She stared around the hotel room. "Why Boston? I thought trafficking would be in places like Florida, Texas, or California."

He nodded. "They are. The fact is, human trafficking rings are operating in most states."

With that the statement, she slumped back against his chest, not wanting to move away from the contact, his presence being so soothing, reassuring. He was big, strong, and indomitable that she couldn't imagine someone like Colin even thinking about kidnapping her from Logan. No one would want to provoke Logan's wrath.

Colin had been a weasel. He'd sneaked around behind people. She still found it hard to believe she'd been carried out in a suitcase. Her mom used to laugh at her when she was growing up, because she'd said she could take her traveling around the world whenever and wherever in a suitcase. It had been a joke at the time. Only now Alina realized how much of one it wasn't. It was an eye-opener to the world around her, showing her how shady it could be.

For the first time, she considered how very vulnerable every single female was. That didn't exclude married women from being victimized, but the former were much easier, particularly when they lived alone. And that was another reason to consider Caroline's offer. At least then Alina wouldn't be living alone, not for a while.

Although she didn't want to give up her independence out of fear. She could see how that was a step down a path she didn't want to take. She wished she could shrink Logan to a pocket-size elf to keep him with her forever—as if needing that security blanket he'd so generously supplied up to now. One part of her knew it was wrong. But the part that had been kidnapped and tied to a bed for several days didn't give a damn. She'd do a lot to keep this man around. He saved her once. The question was, could he again?

LOGAN COULD IMAGINE Levi's reaction. Particularly given his earlier comment about making a spare room available in the house. It wasn't what he'd intended at all. But at the same time, a disappearing act in this case would not be a bad idea. Was it something they could pull off? Hell, he knew they could. It certainly wasn't all that difficult. They could hire a company to come in and clean out her place, donate the furniture she left behind. It would be a simple matter of taking her back with them on a one-way ticket to Texas. That she was looking to move there was something he would call a coincidence, but he knew the rest of his friends would say it was Levi's hero magic happening all over again. Mason, if he ever found out, would be howling with laughter. But then he also would pat Logan on the shoulder.

He wasn't against running with the idea. He was with leaving these assholes behind to take off with her. She shouldn't have to spend the rest of her life looking over her shoulder. He pulled Detective Easterly's card from his pocket and sent a text. "Hopefully Easterly is closer to finding the other three men involved and the missing women. Then Harrison and I want to be involved when they take down this ring and fast."

She stared at him. "Here I am safe and snug, warm and well fed. They could be hurt right now. Or dead."

He rubbed her shoulders. "At least now we know there are other women. For the ones Colin was responsible for, the police have their IDs to track them down. Somebody knows where these women are."

She settled back somewhat, wrapping her arms around her chest. "Part of me wants this whole nightmare to go away. I want to run and never be reminded of it again."

"Understandable, but it's not just about you."

She frowned. "But can't we do something more about it?"

He smiled. "Harrison's outside right now, checking in with Levi, seeing what our next move should be. We'll do what we can while we are here."

When the door opened, Harrison walked back inside, his face serious and determined. "Levi sent a link and access to the documentation on the server." He motioned at the laptop sitting beside Logan. "Bring it up. They've mapped the women's locations, jobs, and given us a JPEG of all their faces. According to Ice all the women run the same type."

Logan set her gently aside as he stood. She sat up to ask, "Who is Ice?"

"Blonde Amazon woman. Hell of an ex-marine helicopter pilot we work with," Harrison said without even looking at Alina, but watching Logan boot up the laptop and login to the server.

Using the code Levi had sent, Logan brought up the files. Once he was in, he opened the map, and they could see Colin had been hunting locally. He tapped the monitor and said to Alina, "Come look."

She came nearer, looking over his shoulder. "Oh, my God! It looks so scary when you see it like that."

"Red dots are where the women lived. Blue are where they worked. The red are scattered around, but still all within the Boston area. But the blues were gathered in four specific areas." The hospital where Alina worked had dots. The university had several. A large assisted-living home had several more. And then the last one appeared to be another medical center of some kind.

She sat beside Logan. "Presuming Colin had some association with these places, it gave him access to roam freely to pick out his victims."

"Yes." Logan opened his email and sent the map to Detective Easterly. Anything they could do to help with the investigation was a good thing. He glanced at Harrison and asked, "Did they find any connection between the women, other than places where they worked, lived, and their general appearance?"

"No. But the workplace is how they were found."

Harrison put on a small pot of coffee in the room, then said, "Another folder in there has the missing person files for each of the women. Ice also made a time line, so we can see how long they've been missing and how much time elapsed between taking each one. Even though they had Colin, that doesn't mean they don't have other people scoping out women. Somebody else, like the dead brother, may be collecting women too."

"We need to contact Easterly or Levi. Find out if the police have any leads on how Joe Lingam died."

"But we know he was shot," Alina said. "Maybe by the same people who shot Colin?"

"Maybe, but it could be completely unrelated. It's hard to say."

"It will be," Harrison said. "I'm sending Levi a text to find out."

Logan opened the other folders. One had the case files. Another one with a time line, which he checked first. They were taking one woman every three to four months. Which meant many had been missing for years. He glanced at the time line. "The first one went back about four years."

Alina let out a shuddering gasp and dropped back down on the bed. She threw her arm over her eyes. "I don't think I want to see any more."

Logan reached across the bed and grabbed her hand, giving it a squeeze. When he went to pull free, she wouldn't let go. "We need to read the missing persons file for every one of these women."

Harrison shrugged. "Send them to me on my phone. Then we can both go over them." Within seconds they were settled in, reading the histories of the missing women.

Logan grabbed a notebook, one left behind from the brother but completely empty, flipped it open to the first page and jotted down notes as he read.

Chapter 11

ALINA OPENED HER eyes to realize she must've dozed off. She rolled over to see Logan still sitting beside her, reading the files on the computer. She yawned, sat up and slipped off the bed.

"How are you feeling?" he asked.

She smiled. "I'm fine. I hadn't even realized I was so tired."

Harrison spoke from behind her. "You'll probably do that for a few days. Shock and trauma sneak up on you. Your body needs to recover, and it'll take some time."

"And thanks to you guys, I have that," she added seriously. She made her way to the bathroom, and after using the facilities, washed her hands and took a careful look at her face. She still had scratches and bruises, blooming deep yellows and greens now.

Her phone rang on the night table, and she returned to the bedroom to answer it. It was her boss. "Hi, Selena." She smiled.

"How are you doing?" her boss asked. "I couldn't sleep thinking about you. I can't imagine what you're going through still. Are you back home? Are you sure you shouldn't be in the hospital still?"

"No, I don't belong in the hospital," she assured Selena. "But I have to admit I'm not adjusting as well as I'd hoped."

"If you need more time off, say so. You certainly have cause," Selena said. "Now when anyone misses work, I'm immediately worried. Take Tracy Evans. She didn't show up today. I'm sure she's fine. But knowing what happened to you, well, it's making me a bit paranoid."

"I'm sure she's not feeling well. She calls off almost once a month, remember?"

Selena sounded better by the end of the call.

When Alina put her phone away, she turned, Logan still reading files. "Did you guys find anything interesting in the women's files?"

Logan looked up. "Some basic similarities. Size and age, body type—the fact that ten of the women were taken either going to or coming from work helps, but not in any big way. They were likely stalked, picked out. The men probably tried to get close to the women, and, depending on the women's reactions, the kidnappers would know whether they would take the women from home or work. Every three to four months one goes missing."

Alina shook her head. "So, because you saved me, it means they're out looking for another one right now?"

"It's quite possible. No way to know who else would be targeted. Colin's friends could have any number of scouts out looking for potential victims."

Harrison spoke from the far side. "And yet they'd keep the ring fairly small, tight-knit, and very well paid. Too many men means trouble. And the ringleaders will have proof of the girls they've kidnapped, in case anyone decides they want out. A job like this, there is no quitting. Which brings us around to Joe Lingam's file. Levi talked to Easterly. They have no leads. They believe it was a drug deal gone bad."

She nodded. "I presume the police are forming a task force, now that they know these cases are all connected."

"That would be the most likely prospect. But it'll be hard to warn every woman with this body type to watch out."

Alina frowned, her mind returning to her recent conversation with Selena. "Or they may already have the next one." Quickly she filled them in on her phone call.

Logan brought up Tracy Evans on Google and searched for an image. Alina leaned over his shoulder. "That's her. She's my height and body shape," Alina added painfully. "But how could they have grabbed someone so fast?"

"Probably because she fits the profile. It is definitely worrisome." Logan brought up his phone and called the detective. He explained about the woman, adding, "Normally this wouldn't be of such high concern, but she is five feet four inches tall with a tiny frame."

She watched the relief on Logan's face. "He'll check on her," Logan assured Alina.

She nodded. "Then considering the hour, is anyone else hungry?"

Both men checked their watches.

Harrison laughed. "She's going to fit right in with the rest of them."

Alina turned to Logan. "The rest of who?"

"Other women we know. I mentioned them to you before." He laughed. "Let's get dinner. A break is a great idea right now."

"Maybe it's because you didn't feed me, or it's the stress, but I am hungry." She stood and picked up her sweater. "To go or can we go to a restaurant?"

"We should be totally fine to sit in a restaurant."

"Good. Where?"

The men rose and grabbed their jackets. Logan asked, "What do you want?"

She linked her arm through his. "I don't care, as long as there is lots of it."

He gave a bark of laughter and opened the hotel door. The three of them walked outside.

At the car, Alina asked, "Do you think Tracy might have been kidnapped? By the same people? And if so, how would they even know about her? Unless they scouted her out earlier like they did me."

Logan was silent, but Harrison spoke up. "If Tracy was taken according to some quota after you were freed, the kidnappers have a deadline to make. Or alternatively, if they already accepted payment for her ..."

Alina felt that punch to her gut. "It's a hard thing to consider that because I was saved, somebody else is going to suffer." Glancing out the window, she realized she had no idea where they were. "How far away is Colin's place?"

Logan turned and looked at her. "Only a few minutes, why?"

"Did you search it?"

They shook their heads, and Logan said, "Not in-depth. The police arrived too quickly for us to do that."

She settled back in her seat. "Although I'm starving, we should check it out. He had to have a list of names of his prospective victims. If there's any chance it's still in his apartment, we should look for it."

The two men exchanged glances and shrugged. Harrison turned the vehicle on the next side street as he said, "We'll give it a half hour."

"I'll contact the detective to get permission," Logan said,

pulling out his phone.

She smiled, pleased with this turn of events. She could hear Logan talking in the front seat but not clear enough to understand the conversation.

At Colin's apartment building no sign remained that the police had been there. On the sidewalk, she forced herself forward. She didn't want to be here, but they had to look. At the apartment door, Harrison knocked. Although they had permission to enter, that didn't mean someone else wasn't inside.

Standing behind the men, she found herself hyperventilating. She'd been a fool to think she could do this.

As Harrison brought out a small tool and quickly opened the door, she slipped her hand into Logan's. When he squeezed her fingers, she immediately felt better. She might be back to the place where she'd been held captive, but she was no longer alone, and the circumstances were very different.

Inside the apartment, Harrison made a quick sweep to ensure they were alone, then they spread out. She headed to the kitchen first. Colin had coffee and food. But only for himself. Why waste spending money on her needs?

She could see signs where the police had been through the place, but she didn't know if they'd found anything helpful.

She started with the bottom cupboard. She went through every shelf and its contents very carefully. She couldn't imagine him going to too much trouble to hide something. He was lazy. This was easy money for him. The bottom shelves were empty. She went through every drawer. One for junk was of interest, specifically because something was jammed in the back. She took it out, carried it to the kitchen table, and returned the drawer to its slot. In the back was a small notebook. Black and a couple inches wide.

She pulled it out to take a look. It was hard to make sense out of most of it until she came to her own name. It wasn't her full name, just her first two initials and last. Her address was there, where she worked and a date—from like six months ago.

At the check mark below, her blood ran cold. Obviously she'd been on a list and had been checked off as accomplished. But below her name were several more marks. She got up and ran to Logan. He turned when she came in, holding out the notebook for him to look at.

"Where did you find this?" he asked.

"It was jammed in the back of the kitchen drawer. I took the drawer completely out to get at it."

Harrison came over and read the name below hers. "Do you know any of the names below yours?"

She read the rest of the page and shook her head. "No, I don't."

Logan said, "We should get this to the police right away. They'll contact these women and see if they are still safe." He turned the page and found four more names.

Alina's finger shot out and stabbed the last one on the list. "Tracy Evans." She gasped. "I can't believe her name is here."

The men exchanged looks as they both pulled out their phones. Once again, she felt useless. Scared of what she'd found. Hoping beyond hope that maybe the other women were safe. She returned to the kitchen to finish going through that drawer, then started opening the rest of the cupboards.

She found one with a boxful of keys and a satchel tossed

inside. The police would've gone through the bag for anything damaging. She pulled it out and checked. Too small to hold a laptop, but she'd seen kids at the university carry similar type bags. She did a quick glance through it, but it was empty. Which was why it was still here obviously. She went through the rest of the kitchen and didn't find anything more.

She went to the hall closet and opened it. More junk, a mop and brooms. Which really surprised her because he didn't seem to be doing any cleaning when he was here. On the upper shelf was cleanser, and above that had more cleaning supplies.

With nothing left to check, she went back into the living room. The men were still on their phones. She headed to the bathroom and gave it a very thorough check, then went to the bedroom. She remembered all of Colin's movements when he ignored her. He'd opened the night table and dresser drawers, plus the closet while she lay here. She checked out both tables, but there was nothing. She looked in the closet; nothing there. She knew there shouldn't be anything left to find. After all, the police would've been through this apartment.

The bed had been picked up, checked over thoroughly and obviously dropped again. It was on its frame on the box spring but askew. She got down on her hands and knees and checked underneath, but couldn't see anything. The bed was on wheels, so she grabbed the frame at the back and pulled it toward the doorway, to look behind the headboard. A part of it fell. As she reached for it, it fell all the way to the floor. An envelope was taped to the back.

She ran back to the living room. Logan had finished his call. "Come see what I found." Back in the bedroom, she pointed at the headboard.

He glanced around the bedroom. "Did you move the bed?"

She nodded. "I pulled it away from the wall. The police had obviously moved the mattresses and already dusted the headboard. We can see fingerprint dust all over it anyway. When I pulled the bed away from the wall, the headboard fell off." She pointed to the floor. "And this envelope was taped behind it."

He pulled out his phone and took several photos and then removed the 9x12 envelope. He walked back into the living room and held it so Harrison could see.

Harrison spoke into the phone. "I'll call you back. Looks like we found a hidden envelope too." He put his phone away. "Let's clear off the coffee table and empty the contents onto a smooth surface."

They were photographs. Lots of them. Most were of the women. All held in the bedroom, or in the suitcase, evidence that Colin had been the one who had taken them. Those who were tied up were bloodied, bruised.

None were of Alina. She sat back and said, "I'm so damn grateful I'm not among that nasty collection." She hung her head. "What's wrong with me? I should be feeling bad for the other women instead."

"All these women are unconscious. These are reprints. And if you aren't here, we have hope that, while you were unconscious, he wasn't up to other stuff." He held up one photo with a woman nude, obviously tied and unconscious.

Alina clapped her hand over her mouth and shook her head. "Oh, my God." She wrapped her arms around her stomach and paced the small apartment.

Logan lined up the photos, recognizing most of the faces

from the files Levi had gotten access to. Logan looked inside the envelope and found one more picture. He pulled it out and dropped it to the table on top of the others. This one was of men.

Harrison picked it up, studied it. "And why the heck does he have this here?"

Logan looked. "Blackmail. In case anything ever went wrong, he had this photo along with all the women."

"So, if we can identify the men in this photo ..."

Alina walked back over to them. "How many are there?"

"Four in the photo. And if I'm not mistaken, they look familiar. As in the ringleaders who were released and disappeared. But the photo is older, so we'd have to confirm my ID."

Harrison looked over at her with respect. "This was a really good find."

She nodded, but didn't feel like smiling. "It's also horrible. A couple of those women don't even look like they're alive."

Logan picked up several and turned them over. "Names and dates. Likely the time he picked them up."

"And something else. A number. This one says sixteen," Harrison said.

"Is that victim number sixteen?" she asked. "Or was he paid sixteen thousand?"

Logan shook his head. "It's too hard to tell what the number represents." He checked them all. They were all numbered. "The first couple have more information though. This one says, 'eight thousand, Jason.' The second, 'ten thousand, Lance.' Two of the first names of the four suspected traffickers. It's quite possible in the early days these are the men who paid Colin directly. All in all, there are four different men's names, matching the four we're looking into. The rest don't include names. There are fourteen photos, each one of a different woman. At least we know that's how .many we're looking for. I was afraid fourteen purses were actually just the most recent missing women."

"Again it's more proof that he was involved. But hopefully these photos are the ones we really can use." Harrison then lined them up carefully, took pictures and then returned them to the envelope. "We should take these to the police." He stopped and looked at Alina. "Do you feel like you've had a good look, found everything there is to find?"

She shook her head. "I never checked his dresser." She ran back to the bedroom, buoyed by the two things she had found. In both cases, they would be hugely useful. They went through all the drawers, pulling every one out, checking inside, around, and behind them, but there was nothing more.

At the end, she asked the men to pull the dresser away from the wall, saying, "I found the envelope when moving the headboard, and the back panel fell off. Maybe the back of this comes off too."

The men did that and then carefully pried off the back. It matched the headboard, so they had to check. With the back removed, they found nothing more.

Still not ready to leave, she headed to the night table, took off the stuff on top and turned it upside down to lie on its side on the bed. She checked it over but found nothing.

Harrison grabbed the other one and did the same. She went back to the headboard, still on the floor, and checked to make sure they hadn't missed anything. Finally, she stood in the room and said, "I don't think anything else is here."

Both men nodded, and Harrison said, "And we would

agree with that."

Logan reached out a hand to grasp hers. "Let's go. We'll drop these off at the police station, then get that food we promised you."

She gave him a grateful smile. "At least now I feel like I earned a meal. I couldn't stand the thought that another woman might be missing, and here I was warm, free, and being fed while she was likely tied to a bed. She probably still is, but maybe now we can track her."

"What we can confirm is she's been taken by the same group of assholes. And her time will run out—soon."

AT THE POLICE station, Logan kept his arm around Alina. It was either that or let her pace until her shoes had holes in the bottoms.

Coming into the police station was unnerving for a lot of people. In her case, it was very understandable. But he thought it was more the realization that another woman had been taken in her place. She'd been amazingly resilient so far. He wanted her to hold on a little longer.

They had to meet with the police, and Logan would keep it as short as possible. After that they'd head off to a restaurant, feed her and then take her back to the hotel. He was hoping she'd go to sleep easily. But he wasn't sure if it was possible tonight.

Last night she'd slept, but that was more about physical exhaustion. He knew she was still feeling incredibly sore, but apparently she was the kind who never complained. And she had no prescription to be filled, so she was handling her injuries without painkillers. That made him respect her even more.

After asking for Detective Easterly by name, they were escorted to a table in a small room. They all took seats on one side and waited. The detective came in quickly with a notepad. When they showed him all the stuff they'd found, he shook his head.

"I can't believe any of this was missed."

But when they explained where the stuff had been found, it helped to mollify his anger.

As they handed it all over, Logan said, tapping the picture with the males, "We think this picture of the four guys is connected to all these women individually photographed. That this is the group of kidnappers and these were their victims. We need to find proof of that though." He spread out the women's photos. "The early ones have men's names on the back. We're really hoping that has something to do with these male faces. If we're lucky, that might be the names to help identify them. A lot of photos have no male names written on the backs."

Detective Easterly quickly went through the photos, then looked at Alina. "None are of you." He looked at each man with a hard glare, as if thinking they had stolen it to protect her.

"I don't remember him ever taking any. I never saw him with a camera." She shook her head. "Chances are he takes his photos and then gets them printed. He didn't have time with me."

The detective dropped his gaze to the pictures and nodded. "That's possible." He picked up the notebook and shook his head. "So many women."

"And under my name is a check mark," she said bitterly. "Nice to know he was keeping track."

Logan leaned forward and tapped the name at the very

end. "This woman is the one I called you about. She didn't show up for her shift at the hospital. Unfortunately, we're afraid she's been taken in Alina's place."

The cop nodded. "Given her physical stature and similar size…it's all too likely. Forensics are all over the suitcase, and they've found hair and in some cases blood. There are also epithelial cells. It's gonna take a while, but we will get to the bottom of it." He glanced over at her. "Where are you staying? And are you back at work?"

She shook her head a little too violently for the occasion, Logan thought. He reached over and grabbed her hand to help her calm down. She took a deep breath. "I stayed the first night at my place. The guys were with me to make sure I could actually get some sleep, but I can't stay there anymore," she said. "Look what they just did. Colin threatened they would come after me. But now that they've taken Tracy, I don't know if they're still after me or not. I want to leave. I want all this to go away."

The cop's face softened. "I'm sorry this happened to you. We're doing our best to solve it."

She reached out with both hands and clung to Logan. "Can I leave town? Go to Texas and stay with a friend there?" She looked at the cop hopefully. "I'm just so scared. I don't want to be alone anymore. I have nobody here."

The cop frowned. "As much as I understand you need to get away …"

Logan butted in. "Unless, of course, you can do a round-the-clock detail for her?" There was no budget for such a thing. "Otherwise we can escort her to Texas and see her settled with her friend there. She should be able to rebuild a new life and hopefully forget this one. She can fly back for the court case."

Detective Easterly frowned, staring at the new evidence in front of him.

Alina squeezed Logan's fingers hard as if to say thank you.

Harrison added smoothly, "Of course we won't be leaving just yet."

Detective Easterly looked up and nodded. "You guys came up with a lot of very helpful information. Not everybody here is very happy about that. But we must find these missing women, and fast. Worrying about egos is not my department right now."

Logan grinned. "It's all right. We understand. We'll do what we can while we're here."

"I had Artie track down the woman's address. We had a black-and-white go over there, but she's not answering her door. Now that I see Ms. Evans's name here, we'll assume the worst. We'll get officers inside her apartment."

Logan lifted that piercing gaze of his and stared at her. "Can you think of anybody else who might've been involved? Any chance somebody you work with might have been helping Colin?"

She shook her head. "I can't imagine. It never occurred to me what Colin had been doing. I never liked him, but still didn't think he was capable …"

The cop's gaze narrowed with interest. "How often would you see him, and how did he try to approach you?"

"He kept asking me for dates, but I kept saying no. Then the day I was kidnapped, I went the cafeteria to get coffee. It was after my shift, and he was there, so I sat down with him." She shrugged. "Honestly, I don't remember anything after that."

The cop nodded. "Chances are he drugged your coffee."

"Because I was snatched from the hospital where I worked," she said in a trembling voice, "I don't want to go back there. All I'll ever do is look over my shoulder."

Logan wanted to add something, but knew it wouldn't help. It wouldn't matter if she went to this hospital or not ever again. It would take a long time to stop looking over her shoulder regardless. He'd known several people who had been kidnapped, and one thing they always felt was that sensation of heading into danger again. They always carried that feeling of having to watch their back to make sure they were safe.

She glanced at the other two men. "But I'll feel so much better when all these missing women are found, especially Tracy. She's the most recent and should be easiest to track, right?"

At that, the detective's phone rang. He answered it; the others waited while he finished the call. "That was the black-and-white. They're at the apartment right now. The door was open. The lock showed signs of forced entry. No sign of her in the apartment."

With that Alina sank back with a cry. Logan reached out and held her in his arms. "Calm down. This is not your fault."

"But if you hadn't rescued me, she would have been safe."

Harrison shook his head. "You can't think like that. For all you know, they were planning on snatching her too. Her name is in the book."

She stared, her mouth open. "What kind of a world do we live in where they'd take women from their homes and put them in suitcases to sell to the highest bidder?"

Logan looked at the cop, but he was phoning someone

again.

"Does the apartment building have security cameras?" he asked Easterly.

He smiled at Logan and said, "Give me a couple minutes. I'm checking." While they waited, Easterly rose and excused himself. When he came back, he said, "Yes, they do. Getting the videos right now to look." He turned to Alina. "I'd like you to watch, see if you recognize the person taking her out of her apartment. Of course, I can't guarantee any decent imagery. But, just in case, would you mind waiting until we can look?"

She bolted to her feet. "No, I don't mind. Yes, I'll definitely look at the video. Anything to help find her."

Easterly took them to another area, where several monitors were set up. He asked her to take a seat, and with Harrison and Logan standing behind, they watched the camera feed. And sure enough, sometime earlier today, a large male, tall, his back to the camera, popped the outside door open and in seconds was inside Tracy's apartment. The recording came with no audio, so they couldn't hear what went on. They fast-forwarded, waiting for the man to come out. When he did, he pulled away a large suitcase on wheels.

"Where did he get that from?" Alina asked.

Logan said, "He probably delivered it to her apartment earlier."

The cameras followed him to the elevators. But he was very careful to keep his face out of sight. He disappeared into an elevator. They switched to a camera inside it, but again, he kept his face out of view. They followed him outside, but it never once caught a glimpse of his face.

He was tall though. And large. She tried to place a physique like that but didn't really see a resemblance to anyone she knew.

He stopped outside on the street, turned toward the first intersection. He looked up, then crossed the street.

Logan asked, "Can you patch into the city cameras from here?"

Detective Easterly called over a different police officer. He sat, shifted programs and on the screen on the right brought up the camera at the intersection. Sure enough, it caught the full face of the man hauling the suitcase.

Logan yelled, "That's it. I know who that is."

Detective Easterly asked, "Who?"

Logan turned to Harrison. "Do you recognize him? From this morning?"

Harrison nodded. "Oh, yeah. That's the asshole who gave us the boxes he had kept after his brother's death." He snorted. "That's John Lingam, terrified to talk to the police, brother of Joe, whose address was linked to the four traffickers."

Chapter 12

LEAVING THE POLICE station and heading for the nearest restaurant that looked good to them all, Alina asked Logan, "Did you mention it to Levi?" This time she was in the passenger seat while Logan drove.

He obviously understood her cryptic question. "Why?"

She shrugged. "I guess I'm wondering when you're leaving. And what your response is to my earlier request." She shot a sideways glance toward Harrison; he was stretched out in the back seat, his legs up, listening. She frowned at him. "Did Logan tell you?"

Harrison nodded. "I can't say I'm surprised."

Her eyebrows rose. "Why?"

"Because in this situation, I'd want to get a hell of a distance away too. And disappearing is something I can do. It would be a lot harder for you without help."

Then Logan's phone rang. "Levi, what's up?"

"One of the four traffickers has turned himself in— Lance Haverstock. He says he and the two other men killed Colin Fisher and Jason Markham, the man you found. The other two are still in the wind. But Haverstock's spinning quite a tale."

Logan stood. "That makes sense. Taking care of any weak links now after being arrested, making sure the cops can't make a case stick."

"We can't afford to assume anything at this point." Levi paused for a moment and then said, "How is she holding up?"

"Scared. Feeling guilty. Otherwise she's doing fine. She's healing, but it'll take time. She wants to disappear in case they should try again."

"Smart of her. Where does she want to go?"

Logan winced. This wouldn't be good. "She has a friend in Houston." He could hear Harrison chuckle from the back seat. And also the stark silence on Levi's end of the phone.

Then Levi laughed. "I guess my intuition was right on when I asked if I'm supposed to make room for her here."

"That shouldn't be necessary. Her friend moved away from Boston a few months ago. I guess they've been very close since they were kids, only Alina wasn't prepared to make such a drastic move."

"And how about now?" Levi's tone was dry. "What should we do to make it happen?" His tone turned brisk. "I presume she has furniture to be disposed of, and the place needs to be emptied, and the lease canceled. What about her job?"

"She's been given several days off, but she's considering telling them she can't handle returning to work after what happened. I'm sure they'd understand and let her walk without any penalty."

"Right. Let me call you back."

Alina watched as he put his phone away.

He shrugged and said, "He'll get back to me."

She leaned over and kissed him on the cheek. "Thanks for taking the chance."

He raised his eyebrow. "What chance?"

"To help. Even if Levi can't do anything about it, I appreciate the thought."

They chose a restaurant and quickly ordered, Logan aware of Alina's need to eat. After they finished their dinner and ordered coffee, Harrison contacted Detective Easterly for an update on Tracy's fate. He hit speaker and laid the phone down on the table so they could all hear the conversation.

"The men went through the place but found nothing. No sign of him or her." The cop was frustrated and angry. "We followed the city cameras, but he must have another hideaway where he can take her, or he delivered her right away. We're still tracking down where he went from his last position."

Logan spoke up. "Make sure you check any properties under Joe's name. The brothers felt a great deal of animosity for each other. Although Joe rented the house next door from John, Joe still might have had another place. He had a lot more cash than his brother knew about too. Also, John had a second property in the Melville District."

"If we can believe anything he said," Easterly added.

"Right." Harrison leaned forward. "Let us know what we can do."

The detective rang off, and the three of them stared at each other. Logan was worried about Alina. The color had washed out of her face. Though she had just eaten, she looked like she was ready to pass out. He covered her hand with his. She barely moved. He glanced at Harrison and raised an eyebrow. Harrison nodded. Not a whole lot they could do but get back to the hotel and keep her safe. They asked for the check.

When they cleared the bill, Logan helped Alina to her feet. Keeping an arm around her shoulders, he led her out the front door. "We have to trust they'll find her."

"I trust that *you* will," she corrected. "I'm not sure about anyone else."

He tucked her closer and held her. When Harrison walked out of the restaurant, the three proceeded to the car, Harrison driving this time. They were only a couple blocks from the hotel.

In the car, Alina asked, "Can we drive past John's place?"

Logan winced. "That's not likely to help."

She stared at him, and the dark wells of emotion in her eyes made it hard for him to argue.

Harrison shrugged. "Why not? Maybe we can figure out where she is. Joe had a place of his own even when he lived at his brother's house. John might have inherited property from his brother or used the cash he got after his brother's death to buy the Melville District property."

"You think he kept it?"

"Why not? It's not like the market has been very good for sellers. And if he had any connection to the business his brother was in, then maybe this was a good opportunity for him to step into his brother's place."

"It's only three women in a year for Colin. We don't know that this brother wasn't also procuring several in that time. Or maybe his brother was a trial run? Or they worked together. We know it was connected. Maybe one was the scout, and then they switched off who got to kidnap the women."

She shook her head. Her voice low, hard, and painful. "I know several women are suffering right now, and I'd like to do anything I can to help them."

Logan had the laptop open, already running properties under both brothers' names. "If it's that obvious, the police would've been there already though."

"I don't think he's a hardened criminal. His brother, yes," Alina said. "I'm hoping he will go home and take his prize with him. What if he had to go somewhere first? And what if he hadn't quite made it home? What if, once he got close, he was worried, remembering you guys had found him, wondering if the cops might come too? What if he then made a sudden decision to go somewhere else? Can they track down his vehicle? Perhaps he knows a citywide search for him has begun. But what about hotels? Has anybody checked them, particularly ones between his place and where he was last seen on the cameras? There's more than a couple, I'm sure."

"Joe did have a small apartment, but it was sold about six months after his death. Apparently, he had rented it from time to time and used the income to live off while staying in his brother's house with various friends. Let me check some of the names out." A moment later Logan spoke again as he read the information flashing on the screen. "Found another property listed to Lingam with the names reversed. So instead of John Lingam, it's Lingam John, and it's only a couple blocks from the house we were at. We're less than two minutes from that property anyway." Logan quickly gave Harrison directions, and within minutes, they pulled in front of a rundown house that looked to be deserted. Several other similar-looking residences were in the neighborhood—ready for demolition or just unkempt, like renters hadn't given a damn. The front lawn wasn't mowed, the front door needed paint, and to have the roof shingles replaced. Maybe it wasn't just the tenants, but also the owners. He studied the property and then drove past and parked.

Logan turned to look at Alina in the back seat. "You want to come or stay here?"

"I'm coming," she said. She opened the door and hopped out.

Logan did the same beside her. He reached out, grabbing her arm. "You stay at my side then." He infused his voice with enough power for her to understand she had to listen to what he said.

She glanced at him and nodded.

HARRISON WALKED AHEAD as if not together with them in any way. He walked to the front and rang the doorbell. The two of them kept well back. When no answer came, Harrison walked around to the back of the house.

Logan's phone buzzed. He pulled it out.

The text from Harrison read **Come to the back**.

With a quick survey of his surroundings, Logan led Alina on the sidewalk that went all around the house. At the back, he saw a fenced yard. The fence itself seemed to be in better shape than the rest of the property.

Harrison stood at the back door and said softly, "Door's open."

The two men frowned, staring at each other, assessing the odds. Logan glanced down at Alina, wishing she wasn't with them now.

As if catching his train of thought, she glared at him. "I'll be fine. Go in and check. Make sure the place is safe."

"Stay here."

She stepped to the corner, out of sight from almost every angle. "Good idea. Go search. See if she's in there."

He ran up the porch steps, and together he and Harrison entered the house. The place was dark and empty. They did a sweep of the first and second floors, but found nothing. No one had been here in a long while.

As they were ready to leave the house, a vehicle pulled around to the side of it. Harrison grabbed Logan's arm. "Go to Alina and get her out of here. I'll stay and see who it is."

Because of the position of this new car, they couldn't leave from the back door anymore. They both slipped out the front, and Logan raced around to the back, grabbed hold of Alina and took her to the side of the property where she couldn't be seen.

She was trembling in shock. "Did you find her?"

"No. A vehicle just drove up, and we have to get you away safely."

She dug her feet in. "It's probably him. We have to see if she's here."

"Cops are on the way," His voice hardened when he added, "I have to make sure you're safe."

She shoved her chin up and forward. "You can't make my safety a priority over another woman's."

He glared down at her. "And that's where you're wrong. I will do everything I can to keep you safe. I will also do the same for her. But we don't even know for sure she's here."

"So, find out," she cried in exasperation. "Stash me somewhere safe and then go."

He gave her a lopsided grin. "And where do you think you're safe?"

And she realized she'd have to go to the car. She rolled her eyes. "I'll lie down in the back seat. I promise I won't sit up, so nobody will know I'm there."

He shook his head. "If anybody's watching, they already know you're here." He opened the back door to the rental and helped her get inside. "Stay out of sight."

He closed the door and then turned to study the house.

Harrison bolted toward him. "Move. He's backing up. Let's go."

"Go, go, go!" Logan raced to the driver's side of the car, Alina right beside him, hitting the unlock seconds before Harrison dove in the passenger seat, and Logan hit the road at top speed. They weren't about staying hidden anymore; they were focused on following John. This was about making sure the asshole didn't shake them.

Logan could hear Harrison's call to the cops, but he didn't take his attention off driving through traffic ahead of them. "Hang on. Make sure your seat belt is buckled," he tossed back to Alina.

"It is," she said in an almost panicked voice. "Don't let him get away."

"I've no intention of it."

Harrison said, "The cops are setting up a roadblock. Helicopter will be in the air in ten. At the rate he's driving, we might have a major car crash."

He could hear the panic in Alina's cry behind him. He reassured her. "Not from us. That guy is driving incredibly recklessly. He's desperate to get free right now. When we catch him, he's looking at twenty years in jail."

"Hopefully more," Harrison snapped. His phone rang.

Once again Logan could hear him talking—he presumed to the cops.

"We've taken two rights," Harrison relayed the directions into the phone. "They got us on satellite now. The request is to stay on him, hoping to direct him toward the freeway, where they are setting up a roadblock on the on-ramp."

Logan watched the getaway vehicle speed through a red light. He was forced to put on the brakes as the cross traffic picked up between them.

Behind them Alina cried out, "He's getting away."

"No, he's not," Logan snapped. "I can still see him ahead of us."

Although this guy was smart, making several turns to lose Logan, no way in hell would Logan let this asshole get away. As soon as the light turned green, he jumped forward, picked up speed past the turning traffic and caught sight of the vehicle ahead. Keeping an eye out, he completely disregarded traffic signs. He pushed the small car to top speed as he slowly gained on the kidnapper.

"The cops don't want you to be right on his tail. If you can, they're asking that you stay back a little." Harrison was back to talking to whoever was on the other end of his phone.

Logan nodded to say he understood. That wasn't quite so easy. He let up on the gas. At a distance he saw an opening between vehicles and moved over a couple lanes. "I think he's headed toward the highway."

"Looks like it," Harrison said. He tapped the laptop. "Stay straight. If we can push this guy to the right-hand turn, a roadblock will be waiting for him."

"Looks like he's about to take the right turn…"

The getaway car, at the very last moment, took a hard right and spun onto the on-ramp. Logan, farther behind, turned easier. They were headed into a roadblock.

"He's not slowing down," Logan's voice rose as he watched the car speed up, racing straight for it. The car clipped the police and kept on going as men dove out of the way.

Logan leaned on the horn, letting the cops know he was coming through as well. Only remnants of the blockade were left. Driving the vehicle hard, Logan went full speed ahead, thankful for a small opening to let them inside the flow of traffic. He was two cars behind. Now he could hear the helicopter.

Alina called out, "It's above us."

"Good. They should keep track of where he's going," Harrison snapped. "If he's fully tanked up, he can go a hell of a long way."

"We have to hope he runs out of gas."

The vehicles between Logan and the runaway transferred over to the center lane, and Logan moved up.

"Several fields are up ahead, all bordered by heavy woods," Harrison said.

Logan barely had a chance to notice the surrounding countryside when the getaway vehicle ahead took a hard right and drove straight off the road into the fields and dropped into a bit of a ditch. But then it bounced down and right up over the ditch and ripped into the high grass, heading for the trees on the far side.

"Hang on," Logan yelled.

He took the angle slightly better down into the ditch and back up on the other side, then turned the wheel and straightened. The other car stopped ahead. As they reached the vehicle, they saw Lingam disappear into the wooded area, showing no sign of a limp.

Harrison called back. "Check the car for the girl." And he was gone after Lingam. Two more police vehicles pulled behind them. Logan told them to start searching the woods. Two men took off on the manhunt; another came over toward the car, and together they popped the trunk and sure enough found the suitcase.

Alina stood bedside them. "Hurry, hurry, hurry. How

much air could possibly be in there?"

The men glanced at each other as they carefully lifted the heavy suitcase out. Logan was surprised at the actual weight. It also gave him hope. They laid it on the ground, struggling to unclip the locks on the suitcase.

"Hurry, open it," Alina cried, dancing impatiently.

Finally the locks gave way, and they threw the lid back.

Inside lay a small woman, curled up tight. Logan shook his head. "Damn, that's a tight fit." And worse, her skin tone was lax, white.

"Let me see her," Alina said. "Move out of the way."

She squeezed in front of the cop and reached down for the woman, searching for a pulse, any sign of life.

The cop protested until Logan said, "She's a nurse."

Then he stepped back and pulled out his phone. "I'll get an ambulance for her."

Alina lifted her face, tears in her eyes, and whispered, "She's alive. Oh, my God! We made it in time. She's alive."

Chapter 13

ALINA CAREFULLY DIRECTED the men to lift Tracy out of the suitcase. That was a delicate operation. She was in so tight, they had to move her joints individually to ease out each limb. When they finally had her free and stretched out on the grass, Alina could work much better. She didn't have any equipment, but she was bound and determined to see if Tracy had any further injuries. Behind her she could hear the men's voices.

The cop said, "The ambulance is on the way."

It was a damn good thing because Tracy's color and heartbeat were incredibly erratic. Alina also found the injection site which pretty much matched hers. As she checked over the woman's body, she was relieved to find no broken bones. She sat back on her heels and stared at Logan. "With any luck, she'll sleep through this whole thing, and not remember any of it."

Sitting down beside her, the cop asked, "She's drugged?"

She pointed to the injection site.

"Yes," Logan said. "She didn't have the same bad reaction you did."

Alina nodded. "Looks like they only injected once. He didn't have her long enough to do much more than that." Under her breath, she added in a heartfelt whisper, "Thank God."

Logan straightened her up and pulled her into a hug. "You did well. We found her, and she'll be okay. Now, you're not to blame, you hear me?"

She nodded, her gaze still on her coworker. "I know that. At least a part of me does. But ..."

He gave her a little shake. "Stop. That's enough. Forget about these guys and go about living your life again."

Alina looked at him and smiled. "Live my life where?"

He motioned to Tracy. "Has finding her changed how you feel about not returning to your job? Do you feel better about your decision?"

She glanced down at the ground. "It helps me leave with a clean conscience," she replied, adding, "but it doesn't change the fact that I went through what I did. And that experience is now tattooed in my brain. I don't know if I'll ever feel comfortable at my place or work, but in some ways, it feels like a chapter closing. No"—she shook her head—"let me rephrase that. It feels like one has slammed shut. Even if I could go back to those two places, I don't want to." She turned in his arms.

"Good enough. I didn't want to unfairly persuade you to move to Texas," he said. "But I'm really hoping you do."

She pushed back slightly, looking at him. In a low voice, very aware of the cops milling around and the ambulance quickly turning off the highway, racing toward them, she asked, "Seriously?"

He leaned forward and kissed her gently on the forehead. "Seriously."

She slipped her arms around his waist and leaned in. Her heart swelled with joy when his went securely around her. She didn't want to feel dependent on him; neither did she want to view him as an escape. Because those things weren't good long-term. And to think she may have found somebody through this maelstrom of horror, well, that made up for a lot. He was a good man.

"We'll get the asshole who kidnapped her," Logan said.

With the ambulance moving toward them, they stepped out of the way. When the men loaded Tracy onto the gurney, Alina turned to Logan and said, "I should go with her to the hospital. I don't want her to wake up alone."

He nodded in understanding. "You've got your phone. Let us know when you're ready to leave."

She nodded and walked toward the ambulance, stopped and turned to look back at Logan. "You'll call me if I can't get through to you, right?" She hated the fear and tremor in her voice, but this wasn't the time to hide her worries. She needed to know if he would be there.

His grin flashed bright. "You're not getting rid of me that fast." But he did ask that a policeman ride with her and Tracy.

She gave him the sweetest smile she could, then turned and climbed into the ambulance. She knew the hospital's policies. She might not be allowed at the woman's side, not being family. But since Alina was there at the time of Tracy's rescue, and Alina had already gone through the same experience, she was hoping the hospital personnel might make an exception for her.

They weren't far from the hospital. She was grateful she wasn't on the gurney this time.

She could see Tracy's vitals as the EMTs checked them. Her heart rate was very slow. Who knew what or how many drugs she'd been given?

The ambulance kicked on its sirens and drove as fast as it could back to the hospital. Alina realized the attendant shared her concerns too.

At the ambulance bay in the emergency area, Alina hopped out first to get out of the way while the EMTs unloaded Tracy. She was rushed into the emergency room, and Alina was left to mill around, feeling left out. She wasn't a nurse in that department, but she'd done several stints there, so she understood the process and procedures. But she'd never been on the other side, waiting for a victim to receive treatment.

She didn't like it one bit. It was unnerving to sit and wait, trusting in others to get the job done correctly. Part of her wanted to race in there, make sure they were doing everything they should be, and another knew she did not have the right. That was their domain. She could say she was a nurse until she was blue in the face. But she wasn't in charge. Finally, when she didn't hear anything, she asked a nurse who had come out of Tracy's room, "How is she? May I sit with her?"

The woman frowned, opening her mouth.

Alina explained how she had been in the ambulance with Tracy, had been there on the spot when she was rescued, and in the same kidnapped situation as the patient. "I don't want her to wake up alone with that nightmare in her head. Please let me sit with her." Then she added, "I don't know if makes any difference, but I am a nurse. I work out of University Hospital."

The woman nodded. "The doctor is about done. When he is, you can come in a few minutes later."

Grateful, Alina said, "Thank you. I appreciate that."

The woman turned to look at her. "You were kidnapped as well?"

"The same human trafficking ring, different kidnapper."

The woman shook her head. "Who'd have thought there'd be such a problem in Boston?"

Alina went in a few minutes later and sat beside Tracy's bed. She reached out and covered her coworker's hand with her own. She knew how important it was for people in a drug-induced state to believe they had a purpose to return, a reason to live. And she wanted to make sure the kidnapper couldn't claim another victim.

"Hi, Tracy. I'm Alina. I was there when the police found you," she said. "Just know that you're safe here in the hospital, and you'll be fine now."

There was no response, but then Alina hadn't expected one.

She stayed where she was, occasionally talking to the comatose woman. A nurse came in to check on Tracy and asked, "Any change?"

Alina shook her head. "No, not yet."

"Let me know if there is." The nurse left her alone again.

That happened several more times. And finally, after the silence shifted in some almost imperceptible way, Alina looked to see Tracy opening her eyes.

"Tracy," she exclaimed. She leaned over and explained once again why Tracy was here. Then Alina said, "I'll be right back." She raced to the curtains and called to one of the nurses, "She's awake."

Within minutes a nurse and doctor walked in.

With a smile the nurse said to Alina, "I need you to step out into the waiting room."

Alina understood what was coming next. She still wasn't prepared to separate from Tracy. She smiled at Tracy and said, "I'll be right outside."

The doctor was with Tracy for a lot longer this time.

When he came out, he walked over to Alina. "She's still confused and doesn't comprehend what happened. I understand from the nurse that you are also a victim. Maybe you can help clarify things. She wants to speak with you."

She smiled at the doctor. "She will be all right?"

The doctor nodded. "Do you have any idea how long she was held for?"

Alina gave him the time line she knew. "A police officer rode in the ambulance with us," she said. "I'm sure he can fill you in with any further details."

The doctor nodded. "She's lucky. There doesn't appear to be any trauma to the body, so we'll take that as a good sign."

"That's good news, indeed." With a smile, she walked past him and went in to speak with Tracy.

Tracy appeared a little more alert. And a whole lot more confused. Alina sat and carefully shared the details of what she knew. The two women had seen each other in the hospital before. Enough to recognize each other's faces, but they weren't friends. And Tracy likely hadn't heard what had happened to Alina.

By the time Alina was done, Tracy shook her head and whispered, "Oh, my God. Oh, my God. Oh, my God."

"The thing to remember is, you're safe. We found you, but I don't know if they caught the man who kidnapped you yet," Alina said. "I know the manhunt was underway when I came in the ambulance with you to the hospital."

And just like that, Tracy wept. She cried and cried. Partly from the drugs, Alina knew; but also from the shock. Alina understood so much of her crying was the sheer relief of having been rescued. And that Alina remembered all too well.

She stayed with Tracy for a long moment. And then Alina's phone went off. She looked at Tracy, patted her hand and said, "I have to take this call. I'll be right back." She stepped out into the hall to see by the caller ID it was Logan. Her grin brightened, and she raced out of the hospital to answer it. "Hey, did you catch him?"

"No, not yet. With the helicopters and about twenty police officers here, he can't get too far."

She groaned. "Damn, I was so hoping. I can't wait to put this to rest."

"It'll happen. How is Tracy?"

"She's awake now. Shocked and grateful to be alive." Alina shook her head as she stared at the setting light outside. "It's going to be dark soon. If he can stay hidden until then, he could get clean away." She wanted to scream in frustration.

"We'll get him. You sit tight. Don't leave the hospital."

She froze, turned around and said, "I'm actually outside right now," she admitted. "I had to take your phone call."

"Get back inside and stay there," he ordered. "I'll text next time."

"Why?" she asked, her fear making her nervous. "You expect him to come back after Tracy arrived at the hospital? How would he know?"

"How can he not? It's all over the news—although the details are sketchy. They said an unidentified woman has been rescued from an apparent kidnapping. She's in the hospital, in the emergency room. Make sure you stand at her side so she can't be taken again. I don't know what the hell's going on. I imagine they must find you and Tracy to make their quota or do it some other way. Losing both of you, they're desperate. They'll be after her, and if they're lucky, they'll find you too."

And just like that, Logan hung up. She cast a nervous glance around and bolted for the relative safety of the hospital. As she walked back to Tracy's side, she realized what he meant. Not only could Tracy be snatched from the hospital, but with both of them here, they could be taken together.

LOGAN TURNED HIS back to the chaos around him. Harrison was still in the woods, tracking down Lingam. The cops were out there too. At the getaway car, Logan looked for any information that would lead to Lingam's associates.

It still bugged him that nobody connected all these missing women. He understood it took several cases before anyone had any inkling something was going on, but to consider the number of women who'd been kidnapped over the last four years, and the cops didn't know? That thought made him view the men around him in a slightly more analytical way.

Logan and one policeman had looked over the car from top to bottom; and forensics was on their way. They'd gone through the glove box where they'd found an old satchel bag, like the one they'd discovered inside Colin's apartment. Once he explained who and what he'd been involved with, the other detectives showing up on the spot had allowed him to take part, if he shared all information. He was thankful because this was a police case, and he really had no business there.

They were currently going through the bag, emptying the contents on the hood of the car, including one smelly sweatshirt. Detective Easterly showed up and told Logan how they had cops working this from various angles all throughout the city. One at Lingam's house, where Logan had collected the boxes. Another at the second residence, where John had driven Tracy but had left in a hurry, as if he knew Logan had been there. The question was, now where would John go? To ground?

Logan really wished they could've gotten this fool before he hit the tree line. But that wasn't to be, and it was pissing Logan off.

He kept glancing around, wondering if the man was hiding in the long brush up ahead, laughing at them. He knew that, if Lingam was smart, he'd be long gone. No way he was getting his car back. And that was just another thing.

"We should check to see if he has a second vehicle registered," Logan said. "Or whether his brother did. He'll need more wheels to carry on from here."

One of the cops stepped out of the way, phone to his ear. That was the good thing about having so many men about. Somebody was always available to track down information. This was the manhunt that didn't dare accept anything less than success. Not if they planned to keep the city safe. They needed to know who was involved in this.

What he really wanted was Lingam's cell phone. "Can we track down his calls?"

"It's in progress. I was hoping something useful would be in the damn bag."

A pocket was in the front. Logan reached in and pulled out a crumpled piece of paper on the bottom. It looked like a hamburger wrapper. But as he spread it out and held up his cell phone to use for light, he could see some notations on it. "A phone number's here," he said.

He quickly turned his phone around and dialed the

number. With the men listening, the phone rang and rang; then a man's voice snapped, "Where the fuck are you? Better get your ass here. You're going to be in deep shit if you can't get that damn girl here fast."

Logan coughed several times, then in a gruff tone, deliberately masking his voice, he said, "Sorry," and coughed again.

"Goddammit, you sick again?"

Logan held the cop's gaze with his as he said, "Just a little."

The man's voice was disgusted. "You better not be on the goddamn drug again. Your brother was a loser that way too. If you want to keep working for us, you'll keep your nose clean and not stuffed with powder."

Holding his shirt half over his mouth, Logan continued to mask his voice as he said, "Be there soon."

The other man snorted. "I don't have time for shit. Things have blown up here. The exchange is tonight. I need the girl, and now. Tell me where you are, and Bill or I will come pick her up."

Logan smiled at the name. This was likely Barry Ferguson. One of the four ringleaders they'd come to check out. The cop held up the name of the mall around the corner. "At the mall. Had to get air in a tire."

"Goddammit, I'll be there in twenty minutes. I don't care how flat your tires are. Make sure you're at the rear right-hand corner where the restaurant is. A gas station is off the main street." Then the line went dead.

Logan held out his phone and said, "Well, that changes things. See if you can track that number." He looked at the car. "We need the suitcase back in the trunk, and we need the car at the rendezvous spot, so he recognizes it."

At that the police galvanized into action.

"It would also be damn good if we had a policewoman inside the stupid suitcase," Detective Easterly said in irritation. "But I doubt I can find one that size that fast."

One of the men said, "Iris. She's small."

Detective Easterly looked at him. "Can you call her?" Then he shook his head. "We don't have time. I have to go through official channels to get this set up."

But the cop was already talking to Iris on the phone. He came back and said, "She's calling her supervisor. We're trying to get this organized. She's on the way in case it's a go."

The men quickly put the car back together again.

Logan realized he was certainly not the physique of the driver. He motioned to one of the cops. "Can you get out of uniform and take the driver's place? You're about the same build as the man we're looking for in the woods."

The cop's gaze shot up, but he nodded and said, "Can't take off my uniform."

"Grab this guy's sweatshirt and pull it over your shirt. Hopefully it's dark enough it won't matter. Besides, we're planning to be there before he shows up anyway. If we're lucky, we'll get more than just him and capture the rest of his network."

The cop did as instructed and turned toward Logan.

Logan nodded. "Rough up your hair and try to look like you've been on coke for the last twenty-four hours."

The guy rolled his eyes. "Great. Just what I need. To copy a drugged-out kidnapper."

"He was angry and pissed at life. Looking to score. Mad that his brother seemed to have found a way to make easy money and took his place from what I can gather. This may be the first time he's taken a woman, and they only used him because Colin was killed."

The cop nodded.

"Let's get going, everyone," Logan said. "I'll take my car to pick up my partner, and we'll meet you there." He pulled out his phone and called Harrison. "Where are you?"

"Heading back to the car. I can see a lot of activity. What's happening?"

Logan quickly brought him up to date.

Harrison whistled. "I'll be there in five. Warm up the car so we can get moving."

Logan ran back to the car and fired it up. They'd been driving through a lot of long grass. The last thing he needed was to have it not run. It was only a rental, not exactly the jeep and trucks he was used to driving. He turned on the headlights and saw Harrison racing toward him while the other men spread out and combed the woods. Logan urged Harrison to go faster. He had the car turned around and his foot on the gas pedal, ready when Harrison bolted into the front seat.

"Let's go."

Logan took off, following the cops. He punched in the location on the GPS. He figured they had about three minutes to get there so nobody saw them arrive. At the same time, he wanted to make sure they wrapped this up tight.

Levi hadn't exactly known what they would get into on this case. Sometimes life wasn't so easy.

Besides, if Logan ended up having a relationship with Alina, well, he'd be more than happy to take her home with him. So he'd considered this an extremely good trip. He knew the guys would bug him constantly, but that was life. He was okay with it.

Up ahead was the turnoff to the mall. He slowed down and headed toward the restaurant. The gas station was at the back, and he made sure they were in position.

The last thing he wanted was to get involved in any more wild car chases tonight with his rental.

Chapter 14

Back in the hospital emergency room, Alina walked into Tracy's room.

Tracy looked up in relief. She reached out a hand and said, "I have to admit, I'm really grateful you're here."

Alina grabbed her hand. She sat on the edge of the bed, "I checked in with Logan, and so far, the man who kidnapped you hasn't been caught. There is quite a manhunt for him right now. But they want us to stay alert, and hopefully they can catch him and the ringleaders before anybody notices you are here in this hospital."

Tracy's eyes widened as she realized the implications. She lowered her voice, looking around hurriedly. "You really think he would try to attack us here?"

"It's always possible, "Alina said. "But why would they at this point? Surely the game is up. They should be cutting their losses and running."

Tracy frowned. "He said something about they were out of time." She shook her head. "He actually apologized."

Alina nodded. "That would make sense. After I was rescued, you were snatched to take my place. You weren't exactly on their list for this go-round." She leaned forward and said, "Is there anything else? Some information that would help the cops find the rest of this ring?"

Tracy lay back on the bed and stared at the ceiling, as if

trying to remember. "So much of it is all a blur."

"I know. If we had a location, a house, if he referred to anything, it would be huge."

"He said something about a truck. As in, we have to catch the truck."

Alina sat back and considered that. "A truck. Like a big transporter? Like they must move you? Moving into Mexico, Canada, or to a private airplane?"

Tracy shook her head. "I can't imagine. I'm so grateful not to be there."

"I know how you feel. I hurt for the other women. They've been gone a long time. The last one was taken three months ago." Alina winced at the concept, but it made a lot more sense. "Then they just put you in a truck and meet up with the others. That could be anywhere from California to Florida. It wouldn't take that long, and traveling by land in a private vehicle, it would be much harder to see a woman either sleeping in the passenger side or tied up in the back of a truck—even a normal pickup with a canopy."

Tracy nodded. "He was quite insistent about the time frame. He said I was his big break."

"That's because his brother, Joe, had been involved before but was killed a year ago. If John had any idea how to get in touch with these people, then he'd have a chance to step into his brother's shoes. Joe was making anywhere from ten to fifteen thousand for each woman. So was Colin."

Tracy looked at her and said something surprising. "Am I worth so little?"

"You're worth an awful lot. And they are paying that much just to one leg of this ring. Imagine what both of us would have been sold off for at the end."

Tracy said, her voice low, "Honestly I don't want to find

out."

Alina shook her head. "Neither do I." Then she turned and stared off. "I was actually held for several days. Although I live in Somerville, I was taken from the hospital where we worked. I don't think I can go back there. It's bad enough to be looking over your shoulder, but to think that I was actually snatched from the cafeteria there ..." She shook her head. "Truthfully, I don't think I can stay."

Tracy nodded. "Right about now, all I can think about is going home to my family in Salem." She shook her head and added, "My mom was right. Big cities are dangerous."

"I think it happens everywhere. We just got very unlucky."

"Why us?"

"Whether they were looking for small women to begin with, I'm not sure. But, being our size, we fit into the suitcases the men moved us around in."

"I didn't think such a thing was possible."

"Well, I was there when they opened the suitcase and found you. And it was quite a job to get you extricated."

Tracy let her breath out. "I'm definitely going home now."

"Did you call your parents?"

"The hospital did. My mom's on her way here."

"Good for you. That'll help you get over this. I'm sure your local town has a hospital too. Apply there."

"That's what my mom said." She cast a glance over at Alina and said, "I'm only twenty-two. To think that my life would have ended in such a horrendous manner..."

"I don't think they were looking to kill us. They were selling us as slaves."

Tracy shuddered. "How can this even exist in today's

world? Things like that shouldn't be allowed."

Adding a note of humor, Alina said, "It's not. But not everybody follows the rules."

Tracy stared at the phone in Alina's hand. "I hope they catch him."

"I hope they catch all of them." Alina glanced around nervously. "I'm constantly looking over my shoulder." She shook her head. "I wonder how long it will take for that to go away?"

"How long has this been going on? How could the police not know?"

Alina leaned forward and whispered, "I was thinking about that. But I don't want to consider that some cops might be involved. Still...it's hard not to wonder."

Tracy curled up in a ball as if that concept was too much for her.

Alina realized Tracy was correct. She really needed to go back home and live with her parents. Return to a life where there had been innocence. She would likely never feel that way again, but at least she missed the couple of days tied up like Alina was.

She settled back in the chair and said, "Just sleep. I'll watch over you."

With a grateful smile, the two women still holding hands, Tracy let her eyes drift closed. Alina wished she could sleep away the next few hours too. But her stomach was knotted, and her nerves were frayed. Every second she kept checking her phone for an update. Of course, they were all busy doing whatever they needed to. She wanted this to be over with. But what she wanted most was to make sure the bad guys were caught.

She settled into her chair, resting her head against the

back, her mind free-floating on the concept that a cop was involved. Most were good honest, upright citizens. But often all it took was one bad apple. And in a position like that, he would have access to so much information. Including the list of names to research. The cop could've found where she lived, who she loved, where she'd worked, how long she'd been employed there, any tickets or arrests. Including the fact she lived alone. If nobody would really note her absence, then she'd be one more missing person. And there were literally thousands of those in every big city.

As she sat thinking about how many of the missing women might be due to human trafficking rings, she was overwhelmed. Then a nurse came and checked on Tracy. She gave Alina a smile and said, "Would you like a cup of coffee? We have some here at the nurses' station. I can get you one if you'd like."

Alina smiled at her gratefully. "Thank you. That would be lovely."

The nurse came back with a cup and handed it to her. "We will be moving her down to a different room on the other end. There has been a large multicar pileup. We need all the beds in emergency we can get. It's a couple doors down on the far side, so expect an orderly to come in and move her soon. Okay?" And she left.

The thought of a multicar pileup made her cringe. That car chase she'd already been in earlier had been bad enough. She hoped Logan and Harrison weren't part of it. That none of the cops involved in this case were. Everyone was trying so hard to catch this guy; it would be terrible if something happened.

To think they had met John face-to-face, and he'd handed over his brother's crap. Playing the innocent … And it had worked.

Now she waited for the orderly to move Tracy. Alina didn't want Tracy waking up on her own. Alina sipped her coffee and waited. Still no update from Logan. She itched to text him and ask how things were, but if he hadn't turned his phone off, she didn't want to be the one who got him in trouble when it rang and gave away his position or something. Not the time for her to be pushing things. He would call when he could.

Then two orderlies came in, smiled at her and pulled up the side rails on Tracy's bed.

She nodded to them, set her cup of coffee down and stood. "I'm coming with you."

The orderly smiled and nodded. "We're only going down a few doors."

"Good. I don't want her to wake up alone."

They took Tracy to a big open room and set her up on the far side against the wall. Alina paced the room until they were done. No chair was here for her, so she leaned against the window and waited.

When nobody came along with furniture, she walked toward a nurse, asking if she could take a chair from the outside hallway into the room. The nurse smiled and told her to go ahead. She grabbed it, walked back to the room and found Tracy still sleeping.

She slipped out into the hallway again and saw a public washroom a few feet down the hall. When she was done, she washed her hands and looked in the mirror. Using a brush from her purse, she gave her hair a quick taming, put it into a braid, tied it off, and gave her face a wash, then headed back to Tracy's room.

Before she stepped back into the large room, one of the

nurses called to her. "Tracy's mother arrived. They want a few moments."

Right. That made sense. She glanced around and decided she should probably go to the waiting room outside emergency then. "If you see either of them, let them know I'm in the waiting room. I don't want to intrude."

The nurse smiled and nodded, then said, "Good idea."

Alina went to the waiting room and sat. Now she wasn't connected to Tracy or Logan. Surely she could do something.

With that thought, she rose and paced. Then decided to walk the hallways. She'd never been in this hospital, but most of them were of a similar construction.

She walked the corridor, determined to wear off some of the festering energy inside. When she came back around to Tracy's room, the door was partially open. She peeked inside to see if her mom was still there but found both Tracy and her mom gone. Her mom hadn't wasted any time in taking Tracy away. Alina didn't blame her, but she'd hoped she'd be able to say good-bye. Dispirited she walked to the nurses' station and said, "I see they left. I was hoping to say good-bye."

The nurse looked up. Only it was a different nurse. She gave Alina a distracted look and said, "Sorry, people are coming and going all the time."

She heard the sirens, and the nurse bolted. Coming in were the multicar pileup victims. Now quite perturbed, Alina walked back to the waiting room and slid down in a chair, the only one left. The waiting room had filled abruptly. She could do nothing to help; all she could do was wait for Logan to contact her. With Tracy gone, she was at loose ends. She pulled out her phone, studied it and wondered if it was worth taking a chance, then decided what the hell. She sent a text to Logan.

Tracy's gone home with her mom. I'm stuck at the hospital. Any idea when you'll be done? After she sent the text, she settled back to wait.

Logan sat behind the gas station, waiting to see if the vehicle arrived to meet up with the cop pretending to be Lingam. The suitcase, now filled with rocks for weight, was stashed in the back of the car. They never did get clearance for the female cop to be part of the sting. Hopefully they wouldn't need her.

So far, the vehicle hadn't shown up. The police hadn't been given much time to get their people organized. They had cops spread out all over the end of the mall. Also, a couple ghost cars were hidden throughout. Too many black-and-whites and people get nervous. Then a vehicle drove up. It looked like a work truck, but it didn't have a canopy over the back. Instead it had what looked like foot lockers. As he eyed the size of them, he realized it was a little too easy to imagine one of these women stuffed into them.

He shook his head, thinking that nobody would even think to check something like that. As the truck drove up and parked on the side, a man hopped out and walked around to the back while another went behind the truck cab to unlock on one of the big storage tool chests. Logan recognized him from the photos. It was one of the four men: Barry Ferguson. That was three down and one to go. The man popped open the lid and lifted out a toolbox tray. A full-size truck and that toolbox was at least five feet long, if not six. They could easily fit a woman inside and cover her up. Well, it wasn't happening this time.

He could see Harrison approach from the far side, walking casually, as if heading to the stores on the other end. He stepped within sight of a couple of the guys looking in his direction, but they didn't appear to notice much. The two guys walked over to the car, slammed on it hard and yelled, "Come on. Open up. We don't have time for this shit."

The cop lowered the window and popped the trunk. The men carefully brought out the suitcase and carried it to the truck.

From Logan's position, he imagined they were ready to open the suitcase. But Harrison came up behind them with the cop on the far side and said in calm low voices, "Get on your knees. Hands over your head."

The men froze. Logan raced toward them. He knew they wouldn't lie down quietly. They were facing lifetimes in prison for what they'd done. No way they'd give up easily.

One of the men pulled a gun. Logan fired first and so did Harrison. Other shots were fired from various angles. Logan hid behind the truck to get out of range. Harrison remained with the two bad guys, now wounded and lying on the ground, but they were still alive, swearing fast and furiously.

Logan came around the side of the truck, only to see another gunman running toward the car. He was afraid for the cop. It was not exactly a good place to get caught. He creeped around the front of the truck and looked, but he was on the far side of the getaway car now.

The cop had the driver's door open and was hiding behind it. But he probably didn't know the guy was on the other side. As Logan raced toward them, the gunman stood, leaned over the car and lined up for his shot. Logan shot him first.

Logan raced to the cop, sighed and asked, "You okay?"

The cop nodded. "Yes, I'm fine, but that was damned close."

Logan walked over to the man. He'd shot him high in the chest and didn't know if he would make it or not. He checked for a pulse. "We need an ambulance here. Three of them at least." He glanced around as the other cops started to come out. "Did we get them all?"

But he could see another policeman peeling off, racing after yet another man. Another cop gave chase from a different angle. Even as he watched, the last man went down under one of them.

Logan walked over to the truck with the large foot lockers. With several cops at his side, he hopped up in the bed. All three foot lockers were padlocked. Hard to tell if any had breathing holes without more light. Grabbing a hammer from the toolbox, Logan broke off all the padlocks. Then raised the lid on each locker. With a flashlight, he shone the light inside.

And found terrified eyes staring at him. In each trunk. A total of three sets.

He heard the cops around him cry out and two policemen joined him in the truck bed. One leaned down and carefully lifted a woman up. He called out, "We need an ambulance. Looks like we found the missing women."

Cheers rang out. The other two were lifted free and lowered to the ground as the men carefully removed the gags from their mouths, untied their bonds, then massaged their joints to get the blood circulating again until the ambulances arrived.

Logan sat on the tailgate of the truck, staring at the ugly spaces where they'd been imprisoned. The thought of Alina transported in a locker made his heart ache.

A cop walked over, holding up a phone, then said, "It's for you."

Logan grabbed it then held it to his ear to hear Detective Easterly saying, "We found him. He went back into his old house. He was ready to jump ship. But we got him."

"That's damn good news." Logan laughed. "Actually, that's the best news I've heard in a long time. We've got three bad guys down here and one on the run. Your men are after him. So, with any luck we can get him too." His gave a happy sigh. "And, as I'm sure you've heard, we've found the missing women, so today has been a great day."

Chapter 15

ALINA, ONCE AGAIN back in the waiting room, heard her phone buzz. She clicked on it to see a text message from Logan.

We've got three bad guys, including Lingam, looking for one more. Found the missing women—all alive and well. Looks like we're wrapping up. I'll call you in about ten minutes.

She smiled. She wished Tracy was still here so she could send her the good news. Maybe she still could. Maybe the nurses had her phone number. She rose and walked to the nurses' station. "I know Tracy left with her mom, and you probably can't give me any personal information, but I forgot to get her phone number, and I heard from the police they caught three of the men involved in the human trafficking ring. I wanted to give her the good news."

The nurses exchanged glances and said, "We can't give out any personal information."

Alina nodded. "That's what I thought. Okay, I'll call my supervisor and see if I can get it from her."

She walked down the hallway to the exit. Once outside she put a call through to Selena. When she answered, Alina quickly filled her in. Selena was shocked at the news. When she calmed down enough to understand, Alina filled her in on the rest of the details, explaining how the cops had picked up the rest of the ring but one, and they were tracking that one down now.

"Tracy was just here. She left with her mom, and I forgot to get a phone number from her. I wanted to tell her they've caught a lot of people, so she'll hopefully feel safer now. Do you have a cell I can send a text to?"

Selena muttered, "I shouldn't. You know that."

"I spent three hours sitting at her bedside talking to her. It was my fault I forgot to get it. But honestly I don't think anybody would mind."

"Fine. But you can't tell her where you got it from." Selena rattled off the number.

Alina wrote it down on the receipt she found inside her purse. "Okay, got it." When she hung up, she added Tracy's number to her contact list, then sent her a text explaining in short form that three of the ringleaders were accounted for, and the cops were chasing down the fourth. Then remembered to shoot her another text regarding Lingam's capture and that it looked like things were wrapping up today.

She wasn't expecting an answer quickly, but when she didn't get one, she fretted. Maybe Tracy was sleeping, or she wasn't even looking at her phone. Having a hard time letting it lie, Alina picked up the phone and dialed. No answer. She let it ring. Finally, a woman's voice came on the line and said, "Shut the fuck up." And hung up.

Alina froze. That couldn't be Tracy's mom. So who the hell answered Tracy's phone? Then the panic hit. She quickly phoned Logan. "I called Tracy to let her know the good news, but a woman answered. All she said was 'Shut the fuck up.'"

She could hear the silence harden on the other end.

"What's the number?"

She read it off for him.

"I'll call you back."

She sat in the waiting room with her cell clenched in her fist, hating that once again she was stuck doing nothing to help. Then she worried. What if Tracy hadn't been taken away by her mom? What if her mom had nothing to do with this? Who the hell said it was even her mom?

She got up, walked to the room where Tracy's bed had been placed and opened the door. The bed was still there, and it wasn't even made yet, but the linens were right there. How could they have moved her? She wouldn't have gone willingly. It would be easy enough to give her a shot, put her in a wheelchair and take her out. But then again, why? Still confused, she kept sorting through the bedding and then froze. On top of one of the sheets, under the blanket, was a needle. She took a picture of it and sent it to Logan, then a text.

I think they got Tracy.

His response was instant.

Stay there. Stay safe.

She'd walked away from Tracy, gone to the bathroom, only to find out Tracy and her mom had gone. How long ago had that been?

She sent Logan another message.

Contact Tracy's mom. Find out if she was at the hospital. Because if she wasn't, then a woman is involved, because a nurse told me her mom was with her. I didn't see or meet her.

She wandered to the window, searching for any sign of Tracy, her fists clenching and unclenching in a rhythmic motion as she waited for somebody to get back to her.

Finally, her phone rang. She raced out of the hospital at the rear parking lot and answered it.

"Her mom is on the way," Logan said, "but she hasn't arrived in Boston yet. It wasn't Tracy's mother."

Alina flopped down on one of the benches. "Oh, dear God. I didn't get a chance to see who was with her."

"The hospital has video cameras. We'll get a visual on her within minutes. The police are already patching it through."

"Thank God for that. I'm such a fool. When I came out of the bathroom, I heard her mom was in with her, and I should leave them alone for a few minutes as they needed privacy, so I went for a walk—I wasn't gone ten minutes."

"You are not responsible," he snapped in her ear. "Got that?"

She nodded. "I got that. I'm not, but somehow I feel I am." Of course she understood that was the same refrain she'd already said several times over. She shook her head. "Are the kidnappers' lives actually on the line if they don't deliver somebody? And is she the easiest replacement they know of?"

"It could be any number of things. But we've got the truck with the driver and somebody else. There was a backup vehicle too. We got it. The last man isn't getting away either."

"And who the hell was the woman?"

"The missing link."

He rang off, and Alina sat still for a long moment. Then she went back to the nurses' station and said, "The police are going to be here any minute, but that woman who said she was Tracy's mother has effectively kidnapped her. The police have contacted Tracy's real mother, and she is enroute, but she is not in Boston yet."

The nurses stared at her in shock; no one knew what to say. Or dare not say anything.

Alina could understand. They'd let a patient be kidnapped. The PR storm over this would be horrific. Their jobs could even be on the line. She leaned forward and said, "Please, do you remember what she looked like? I wasn't here when she arrived, and a nurse told me not to go in, so I didn't get a chance to see her. The police will look at the video cameras, or maybe they can do that from the station." She shook her head. "I don't know, but can you give me a description of her—anything to tell me what she looked like?"

One of the nurses lifted her cell phone and said, "I can do better than that. I took a picture of the chaos when the big accident came in," she confessed. "My boyfriend doesn't think it ever gets crazy here. I'm not actually in the ER on duty, but I wanted him to see."

She pulled up the photo, and sure enough, it was a full-on nightmare at the hospital. Paramedics were everywhere, and beds were moved all over the place. And jammed up against the reception counter was a woman, her hair pulled back in a bun at the nape. She was well dressed, a stranger.

"Can you send me that image please?"

The nurse nodded. Alina brought it up on her phone and sent it to Logan.

This is her. Accidentally caught in a photograph in the hallway.

She headed out the back exit with the woman's image strong in her mind. There was a huge parking lot. But how would the woman have gotten an unconscious Tracy into a vehicle? That couldn't have been easy. Unless she had help. Had the woman managed to get Tracy straight out of the hospital, or was the woman hiding somewhere inside?

Amid this much chaos, she could have done any number of things.

Alina raced to the parking lot. "Dammit, where are you, Tracy?"

Of course there was no answer. Her phone rang. It was Logan. "The woman's well-known to the police. They sent out an alert looking for her and Tracy. We also have a vehicle registered to her. With any luck, we'll get her."

"I'm not feeling the luck very much now," Alina said. "She can't have left the hospital more than twenty minutes ago. The cops need somebody in the air looking for the vehicle."

"I'm sure they'd like to. It doesn't mean they have the manpower."

She shook her head. "This is ridiculous. That woman came in and walked away with Tracy, with absolutely nothing and nobody stopping her."

"Hospital administration will have to look at that. But because you got the face, we now know who we're looking for."

Tracy walked to the far side of the parking lot, her rage so extreme her footsteps gave off a staccato sound. "She could still be here, you know? How could the woman get Tracy into the vehicle on her own? Tracy's small, but she's still a dead weight if she's unconscious. And it's obvious she's been drugged again, so what the hell?" she cried out in her frustration.

"Look for a black Honda Civic." He rattled off the license plate. "We're only minutes away."

She heard the letter *C*, but the rest of it went over her head. She spun around looking for black cars. "Do you have any idea how many black cars are here?"

"She'll likely be driving carefully to not bring attention to herself. It wouldn't have been easy to get Tracy out of the hospital and into the car, so she's probably still there. Cops are on the way."

As she turned around, she said, "A black car, a Honda, is heading to the exit. I'm running toward her. I must confirm Tracy is in there."

There was a lot of traffic, and no one would let her vehicle in.

"She's trying to make a left turn onto the main road here but can't cross."

Coming alongside the car, Alina saw Tracy collapsed on the back seat. "It's her. Goddammit, it's her." She opened the passenger door.

The woman hit the brakes and shouted, "Get out. Get out."

Instead, Alina jumped inside and came up fast, slamming the woman against the glass of the driver's side window. The steering wheel jerked to the side, sending the small car to the curb. Alina didn't have any fighting skills except for her pure rage at watching this goddamn woman stealing poor Tracy all over again. Her ire knew no bounds. She kept hitting and hitting and hitting. The woman screamed, fought back, but Alina was like a bedeviled animal.

She could hear Logan in the background, shouting at her from her cell. Yet, she couldn't say anything. The outlet for all her rage, fear, and torment was to keep hitting the woman. When Alina finally drew a shuddering breath, she realized the woman's face was bleeding, and blood was all over the side window. Alina could hardly breathe.

With her left hand, she picked up her phone and gasped. "Oh, my God, I killed her. I think I killed her."

"Stay calm. Where are you?"

She gave him the details.

"Is the vehicle still running?"

Realizing they were sitting in an idling vehicle, she reached over and pulled the keys free. At his instruction, she pulled up the emergency brake to stop them from moving.

"Stay right where you are. We're on the way."

She shook her head. "We're blocking traffic. Oh, my God. What have I done?"

"You've done exactly what you needed to do to save Tracy. Now stop thinking about it. Do not leave the vehicle. Do not leave Tracy. And if that woman gets up, hit her again. Do you hear me?"

She gave a shuddering breath and broke down. "Oh, my God! What am I?"

"You're an animal in pain, sweetie, that's all. You did what you had to. I'm already on the way toward you. I am not very far away. Give us five minutes. Hold on for five more minutes, and we'll be there."

She stared almost blind out at the traffic. Vehicles were going around them. She couldn't look at anybody. She couldn't even begin to lift her face. And then some of her training took over. She reached out with her bloody hand and touched the woman on the neck. Relief flowed through her as she felt a pulse. "She's alive." And she burst into tears.

LOGAN SWORE UNDER his breath. The cops drove ahead,

leading the way as fast as possible. Harrison drove their car with Logan as a passenger. And like him, Harrison was having a hard time keeping behind the cops, wanting to race ahead. "She found Tracy lying in the back of the vehicle. She's beaten the woman driver to a pulp."

Harrison raised an eyebrow and said, "Holy shit."

Logan leaned back and closed his eyes. "Yeah, that's an understatement."

"Is the woman dead?"

"Alina said she is still alive. She's pretty unnerved over what she's done."

"I understand that. I've seen women do some pretty scary things when they're afraid. We're all capable of killing in the right circumstances."

They pulled up to the hospital, coming in through a different entrance, Logan exiting the car before Harrison rolled to a stop. The cop ahead of them drove to the far corner where he could see the black Honda Civic parked. Two other cop cars came in behind them. Others were driving around the stalled car, merging into the traffic on the main lane. Not sure what he would find, Logan raced forward, his hands out to the cops. "Let me talk to her."

Sure enough, Alina sat in the front seat, covered in blood. A woman sat in the driver's seat, her head against the driver-side window, bloodied from top to bottom, moaning.

He opened the passenger door. "Alina, take it easy."

She turned, and he could see the shock in her face, the deadness in her eyes.

Finally, she registered who he was, and lifted her arms like a two-year-old. He wrapped his arms around her and picked her up, taking her out of the vehicle. The cops surged in with a doctor and several orderlies pushing a stretcher from the hospital. With her in his arms, the two of them watched as Tracy was carefully removed from the back seat, and the woman driver was carried on another stretcher that arrived soon afterward.

Alina whispered, "I hope she's gonna be okay."

"I hope she is too. So she can spend a lot of years locked up in prison. Come on. I'm taking you inside to get that hand looked at."

She gave him a broken smile and held up her bruised, bloodied hand. "I guess I'm not going back to work for a while."

"Honey, you're not going back to work until you find a new job in Texas."

She glanced at him. "How could you want to possibly help me after this?"

He leaned down and gave her a kiss on the temple. "Not only do I want to, I don't have any intention of letting you go. Not often do we see people with the character willing to go the distance and do what needs to be done to save others. You jumped into my heart when I first met you. You were so valiant and strong. Nothing that has happened since has changed my mind."

Laying her head against his shoulder, she whispered, "So you only want to be with me because I'm some honorable Amazon woman?"

Logan grinned. "Because you're sexy, and the sweetest girl I've ever met. Because I really want to take you to meet my mom and all my friends." His grin widened. "And because you're some honorable Amazon woman."

She cast him glance, and her eyes were huge. "Really?"

He heard the hope and fear in her voice. He shifted her in his arms and kissed her full on the lips. "Absolutely."

Chapter 16

THE REST OF the day and evening was awash in chaos. Not only did she have to be treated again, but the police were all over her. And through the entire process, she held a deep hidden fear that she'd beaten up an innocent woman. Yet, in her mind, she kept seeing Tracy stretched out unconscious on the back seat. If that woman was innocent, why was she moving an unconscious woman?

Since finding her in the car, Logan hadn't left her alone. He was either carrying her or had his hand in hers. Making sure there was physical contact between them. And she was just as bad. Anytime he made a move, she reached for him. Thankfully, he'd always reached back. She didn't understand this bond.

That it was born through danger was one thing she'd like to think would strengthen as they discovered who each other was. She wanted to believe what they had was something to grow, build, and nurture. She knew he felt the same way, but this was new. And as such, it was like a young sapling springing roots. Something to be protected. To be watered and given sunshine and nutrients. Something that would grow strong, straight, and true over time.

That's what she wanted for their relationship. She wasn't sure how to give him exactly what he needed. She'd never made it that far. All her previous ones had broken up after a few months. Never had she felt about the men the way she did Logan. He'd been her hero and had been there for her every step of the way. She knew she'd make that move to Texas now, without any qualms. Just to be close to him. Just to give this, whatever *this* was, a chance.

At the same time, she had a lot of nightmares to deal with. Not the least of which was finding out that, within her own inner core, was a savage animal determined to protect somebody so much less fortunate when needed.

She'd seen women, mothers, do the same thing when protecting their children. So she shouldn't have been surprised. But she'd never seen that in herself before. Tracy certainly hadn't been her child, but she felt responsible. And seeing her taken once again, had been too much.

The police were all over the damn hospital. She was sure the staff was waiting for them to get the hell out of their lives. She'd had evenings like that. The hospital was overwhelmed with patients from the multicar pileup. Some were taken to surgery, and others were moved in, registered and taken to different floors and specialty areas.

Once again, she was here. Her hand was looked at, and the doctor sent her for an X-ray. So far nobody mentioned the woman. And she was terrified she'd hurt her permanently. With Logan holding her left hand, he led her toward the X-ray room. She sat on the chair and waited. He held the paperwork in his hand, and they sat in silence. When Alina couldn't stand it any longer, she asked, "How bad is she hurt?"

He didn't pretend to misunderstand. "I don't know. They're working on her."

She let her breath slowly escape. "That could mean anything."

He squeezed her fingers. "Yes, it could."

"Am I going to get charged?" She rolled her head to look at him, to see his beautiful green eyes staring at her. "How is it I haven't even noticed what color your eyes were before?"

He shook his head. "No reason why you should. You were protecting yourself and saving Tracy from a human trafficking ring, of which you had already been a victim." He smiled. "And no judge in this country would convict you for beating up the kidnapper to save the victim."

But that was his version. Until she heard that from the cops, she knew she wouldn't relax. Finally, she was taken in, her fingers very carefully spread out into various positions as they took numerous pictures, and she was led back into the waiting room. Logan was there. She sat, and her hand started to really hurt. She'd tried hard not to cry as they had positioned her fingers for the best pictures, but it had hurt. She looked down at her hand and said, "I'm pretty sure a couple of my fingers are broken."

He nodded. "If they are, they are."

She tossed him a smile. "It's my right hand. I do everything with it."

"Especially punching," he teased. "That means no more for you."

She rolled her eyes. "If I knew how to punch properly, I wouldn't have broken my fingers."

He chuckled. "I was going to mention that, but I figured I'd save it for another time."

"I wouldn't mind learning self-defense," she admitted. "When I was tied up on the bed, you can bet that's one of the things I regretted not having learned."

"We can work on that too. Everybody at the compound is high up in martial arts of one kind or another. We do hand-to-hand combat because of our work. We're all trained with various weapons."

She stared at him. "Compound?"

"Where me, Harrison, and the others live and work."

She nodded. "It seems like such a different world to what I know. You kill people, and I heal them."

He smiled. "Then we're a perfect fit."

She sagged against him as they waited for the results of the X-rays. "I hope you mean that."

The radiologist walked out of his office and said with a smile, "You did quite a number on your hand and wrist, my dear. A cast is definitely required. You broke two fingers, fractured your wrist and a couple small bones in the base of your hand."

She winced, glanced down at her hand and said, "I knew it hurt but hadn't realized how bad."

"It'll take a few minutes, but we'll get it taken care of. So you won't be going home anytime soon. Hand this to someone at the nurses' station."

She winced. "I understand the drill. Thanks very much, Doctor."

He nodded as Logan led her back to the main reception room and handed one of the nurses the X-ray report. The woman nodded and said, "Figured it was broken. Okay, let's get you down to one of the treatment rooms. Not sure how long you'll have to wait. It's still really crazy."

"Thank you," Alina said giving him a small smile.

Logan looked at her as she sat on the stool in the treatment room. "You want me to get you coffee or something to eat?"

She shook her head. "I want this over with. We'll talk about food afterward. Now I'm feeling a little bit on the queasy side. The pain from having the X-rays is... Wow. I hadn't really thought about it before, but rearranging broken fingers so they can take pictures is... not fun."

He leaned down and kissed her on top of her head. "But you were so valiant."

She shot him a look. But he appeared perfectly serious. "You got it bad," she muttered, "if you think that."

"I do think that." When his phone went off, he pulled it out. "It's Harrison. I need to take this."

She nodded, already feeling the pain of separation. "That means you have to go outside the hospital."

As he stepped toward the door, he turned and looked at her. "You going to be okay?"

"Did you get all the bad guys?" she countered.

He nodded and said, "You should be safe now."

"Safe. I hope so. Especially if it will prevent anybody else from being kidnapped again." She lifted her broken hand. "This is going to stop me from doing a whole lot."

He chuckled. "Actually, it won't. Once that has a cast on it, it'll really be a weapon."

She brightened. "Then send the doctor in here and get this sucker fixed."

It'd been a shaky couple of days. But he was a hell of a light at the end of the long, dark tunnel. Then she smiled at that. Did he even know what her name meant? *Alina* meant *light*. She'd asked her mom about it a long time ago, and she said her birth had been a light after their journey.

That's how she felt about Logan. He was her light. She'd have to tell him about it later.

And she had no idea what *later* would mean. Were they going back to the same hotel? Were they flying out? With this stupid hand, she'd have an even worse time moving. She didn't even know where to start.

First, she needed to hand in her notice. And cancel her lease. Her mind filled with all the logistics of moving. At the same time, she needed to relax. It was her right hand. While she waited, she tried, with her left, to send a text to Caroline. It was a bit garbled. But Caroline appeared to understand. And her demands were clear, something along the line of **Get your ass over here**.

Alina smiled. She put her cell away as the door opened to let in the same doctor who had examined her earlier. She asked, "You can put the cast on now?"

He smiled. "Sure, if you're ready. It's been a hell of a night so far."

The next few minutes were spent getting her arm bundled up in fiberglass.

"I understand you're a nurse. So, you know how to take care of this, what to watch for, should a problem arise."

She nodded. "And hopefully I won't be alone overnight, so I'll have someone to watch over me, to make sure I'm doing okay."

"If the man pacing outside the door right now is yours, he won't be leaving you to sleep alone. That's for sure."

She felt a smile climb her face. She couldn't think of anything she wanted more than to be sleeping with Logan tonight. Even if it meant Harrison was in the hotel bed beside them. She just wanted to be held. To wake up and know she was safe and sound, and, even more important, that he held her close because he wanted to.

LOGAN WAITED UNTIL the doctor opened the door again, saying, "She can go home now. She needs to keep an eye on

188

those fingers for swelling. The next forty-eight hours are important." And he turned and walked away.

Logan got his first look at her standing there. She sported a bright purple cast on her right arm and over the bulk of her fingers—just the tips were showing.

She straightened and smiled at him. "I don't know where we're going from here, but food and a place to crash would be awesome."

He nodded. "Coming right up."

"The doctor had more good news," she added as he held her left hand, walking her outside. "They put a rush on the rape kit and apparently it came back negative. Also, the drug Colin gave me was a common date rape drug. No long-term side effects, thank heavens."

Logan wrapped an arm around her and held her for a long moment. "That is good news, indeed."

Stepping back, she looked around. "What vehicle are we driving?"

He pointed. "I have the rental car. Harrison came with me, then took a cab to the airport. He's heading to another job. As this has concluded, Levi's ordered us both home."

He watched as her face fell. Helping her into the car, he reached around and got her buckled up. He knew that, for quite a while, she would need help. She was also prickly and stubborn and wouldn't take kindly to being looked after.

"I guess we knew that time was coming," she said sadly. She sank back against the seat and closed her eyes.

He drove back to the hotel and helped her into the same room they'd been in before. Only this time it was just the two of them.

"What about you? Are you going back tonight too?"

He chuckled. "No. I'm staying here for three days.

That's as long as I've got."

"Why do you have that?" she asked cautiously.

He gave her a grin. "Because I asked for them. I figure that's how long it'll take to deal with the contents of your apartment, get you packed up, purchase your airline ticket and, if you have anything to ship, get that done too. We'll have to work our asses off though, if you plan on flying home with me. Alternatively," he added, "we could drive your car. It will take us a while, but we'll get there that way too."

She grinned. "I really could use my car in Texas," she admitted. "And I don't know if we can make all that happen in three days, but I'd sure like to give it a good try."

"Good. First things first—food. I placed an order with room service, and then it's crash time. You need sleep."

She nodded. A knock came at the door. "That was fast."

He laughed. "I called it in from the hospital. Once I realized you were getting a cast, I could give them a time frame."

He opened the door, accepted the trays on the trolley, paid the man a tip, closed it and turned, saying, "I wanted it to be ready. And then you get some sleep. Because tomorrow will be a long day."

While Logan brought the tray over, she sat on the bed and thought about all she had to do. "It doesn't have to be. I'm not caught up by having tons of possessions I must keep. Besides, it's limited to what the car can hold. As for my furniture, it can go to someone else." Taking in the aroma of their meal, she felt her stomach protest its emptiness. "The food smells wonderful."

She readjusted her position on the bed, propping herself against the headboard. He brought her a plateful of food. By the time she had eaten, the effects of shock were wearing off. She excused herself and went to the washroom.

She let out a small gasp at her face in the mirror. She opened the door. "You let me walk around in public like this?"

He took one look at her and smiled. "You're beautiful no matter what."

He went into the small room, grabbed a washcloth, soaped it up in warm water and carefully washed her face. He took a minute to clean the strands of hair along her face, still covered in dried blood. Then he turned her to look in the mirror. "Better?"

She smiled and said, "Yes. I'd love to do these fingers now."

He turned the warm water on to run over the tips as she let them soak underneath the tap for a few minutes. They were still so sore that she didn't want him to dry them. She let them hang to drip-dry and said, "That'll do." When they went back into the main room, he put their dishes on the tray, took it outside the room and left it on the floor in the hallway. Then he came back and said, "Bedtime for you." He pulled back the covers and looked at her. "What do you want to sleep in?"

She winced and stared down at her clothes. "This is easiest."

"You can't sleep in those." He picked up her bag and put it on the spare bed, quickly opened it and pulled out the nightgown she'd worn the previous night. "You up for getting into this?"

She nodded.

Gently, treating her like a little child, he undressed her with complete tenderness.

When the nightgown dropped over her head, she smiled at him. "You'd make a great father."

He shook his head. "Now that's a long way in the future."

She crawled under the covers. He bundled up all her dirty clothes, tucked them into the side pocket of her bag and reached for his laptop, placing it on the spare bed.

She looked at him and said, "Can you turn the lights"— she snuggled farther under the covers—"off?"

HE WATCHED AS she drifted under sleep's embrace. It had only taken seconds. He watched her eyes slowly close. She was exhausted. Shock was like that, and so was injury and pain. He grabbed his laptop and phone to check up on the world, to see if he had any messages. He found an email from Detective Easterly.

Instead of responding the same way, Logan dialed Easterly's number and waited for him to answer.

"Logan, glad you called. I heard about Alina. How is she doing?"

Logan gave Detective Easterly an update on her condition, explaining she was fast asleep right now with her cast elevated. He stood, walked over to her.

"She really went to town on the woman."

"Yeah. How bad?"

"Broken nose and cheekbone, plus a concussion. But she'll survive."

"I have to ask this next question for Alina's sake. Can you confirm that this woman was involved in the trafficking?" Logan reached over and gently stroked Alina's shoulder while she slept. "She was really concerned she'd attacked the wrong woman."

"You can definitely put her mind at ease on that point. It appears she was one of the coordinators in the group. We also picked up the last man, Bill Morgan. The woman is talking, so with any luck, we'll pick up the entire network when we do a full sweep."

Logan reached up and pinched the bridge of his nose. "I sure as hell hope you can track down that system and help recover the missing women."

"The superintendent is setting that up right now. The female coordinator's name as it was on Colin's cell is Roma Chandler. She is giving names, dates, places, and the whole line up. She was originally trafficked herself. So on one hand you can kind of understand, but on the other, well, it's like the worst thing possible. With any luck, we'll find these women. But you know it won't be a fast solution. A warrant has been issued on the house you asked me to look into. We're hoping it's involved in this mess, but it's too early to tell. Also…" He lowered his voice. "A couple names from Roma indicate a law enforcement connection—confirming Colin's mention of two bad cops. That will take even longer to sort out."

"Have to admit, we wondered about that last bit," Logan said. "No, it's never fast tying up something like this. I know my boss would want me to extend all the help we can give. We have connections around the world."

Detective Easterly's voice was light. "That's really good to know, because it looks like this is going all the way around the world. I've asked to be assigned to the task force. Watching how they move those women, that was scary. My sister is about the same size. And thinking of Tracy Evans curled up inside that suitcase is terrifying."

Logan nodded. "At least we saved the ones we could."

"There is that. John also confessed to killing his brother. He was pissed about Joe not paying rent," Easterly said. "Goes to show that you should never piss off family. Speaking of, are you heading out tonight?"

"I'm helping move Alina to Texas. She's got a friend there she'll stay with. She doesn't think she can handle being here anymore. She's not running away from you though, so if you need her for court or deposition testimony, then we'll send you the address once we get her relocated."

"I'm glad to hear that. That woman's got a lot of grit. And that is never a bad thing." The detective ended the call.

Logan thought about that and said quietly to himself, "Grit, that's exactly what she's got."

Beside him Alina murmured, "That's what my grandma used to say."

He laid his cell on the bedside table, sat gently on the bed, wrapping his arm around her, tucking her against him. "You're supposed to be asleep."

"I had a power nap," she said with a half smile.

But her voice was drowsy, as if she was still looking at going back under. He gave her a gentle hug. "Go right back to sleep."

"Not sure I want to," she whispered. "It was really nice to hear you say you are helping move me to my friend in Texas. Clearing the pathway so I could start over."

"I'm a nice guy."

She rolled over under the blankets and wrapped her good arm around him. Holding up her injured arm, she said, "I knew that the moment I laid eyes on you." She pulled his head down and kissed him. "Thank you for the rest of my life."

He placed his fingers on her lips, gently teasing her. "I was hoping you'd be willing to spend the rest of your life with me."

She smiled, tears coming to the corner of her eyes. "Are you sure? We hardly even know each other."

He slid his hand up her body, gently cupping her breasts, his hand still over the blanket. "True, but I know what counts. I know you have heart. I know you'll stand up for the underdog and will defend our children to the death. You're adorable when you're riled. And I admire the honesty I see inside you. What is there not to love?"

A tear sparkled on her eyelashes. She slid her finger across his lips and then pulled him down closer, gently kissing him, dropping little ones on his upper lip, then his bottom and square jaw. As if she didn't know what to say but wanted to show him instead.

And he was willing to accept a demonstration. With a smile, he let her gently explore his face, running her fingers through his hair, stroking down the side of his cheek with her fingertips.

She whispered something across his ear, and he chuckled. "Now that tickles."

She opened her eyes, raised her eyebrow and smiled. "You think that tickles? I might be handicapped because of my bum arm, but that doesn't mean, down the road, I might not take full advantage of you when you're helpless and see how ticklish you are everywhere."

He gave her a wicked grin. "One day down the road," he promised, "you can do what you want. But right now, you look after that arm."

It was her turn to flash a wicked smile. "So, are you going to lie here and let me do my worst?" she teased.

He chuckled. "Well, I don't know about just lying here."

With her good arm, she pulled him down. "I don't think that's possible. Something about you makes me ache to have you deep inside."

At her words his head lowered, and he crushed his lips against hers. He couldn't imagine not wanting this woman in the future. So much about her was perfect. But even if she wasn't, it was like his body knew her, and his heart already recognized her. His soul opened, enjoying her, as if seeing somebody he had already known and was reacquainting himself with. He didn't even know how to explain it.

But thankfully, no words were necessary. When he ripped the blankets off the bed and turned to face her, she shook her head at him and held up her hand. "Oh, no, you don't. You're not coming back to bed unless you strip down."

He gave her grin. "What about you? You're still wearing a nightgown."

She grinned back. "And it's gonna take you to get it off me too."

At that he laughed out loud and quickly divested himself of his shirt and pants. By the time he kicked off his shoes and peeled away his socks and stood before her in his birthday suit, she was on her knees, trying to hike the nightgown over her waist.

He chuckled. "Let me."

Obediently she put her arms up, and gently he worked her bad hand and arm out of the nightgown, then threw it over the side of the bed.

When she was again kneeling before him, he said, "If I'd realized this is what you wanted, I wouldn't have put you in the nightgown in the first place."

"I thought about it," she said, "but I was a little too tired."

"Thank God for power naps," he said in a fervent whisper.

And knowing she was still sore and banged up from her own captivity, not to mention the beating she'd given the poor woman today, Logan stretched out beside her and gently caressed and teased her until she was writhing with passion. Honest in her response. Open in her joy. And he loved every second of it.

His fingers stroked and caressed, teased and delved, and he found he couldn't get enough. He leaned over, his lips and tongue leaving wet trails over her ribs, up to her beautifully plump breasts. When he took one nipple in his mouth and suckled hard, she cried out, her body arching under him.

"God, you're so beautiful." He turned his attention to the other, not wanting either to feel left out. At the same time, he slipped one hand to the curls at the juncture of her thighs, finding the moisture from within. He groaned, sliding higher up her body to take her lips with his. "So responsive," he whispered again.

She wrapped her good arm around him. The cast was cold on his back, but he didn't notice for the fever burning through him. He slid a hand down her back to one cheek, spreading her thighs wide, hooking her legs over his hips in position. He looked down at her and whispered, "Ready?"

Alina smiled and pulled him closer. "I am," she whispered, "I was born ready—for you."

He surged deep inside, closing his eyes as she held him tight within her. She cried out as he seated himself right at her core. And he stayed still, frozen, inhaling the moment. Her muscles eased and then clamped tight around him. He groaned hard. And she did it again.

"You're killing me."

She chuckled. "How about we kill each other—with love."

He lowered his head and whispered, "Absolutely." He took her. His hands slid down to hold her hips firmly in position as he slowly raised and lowered, driving them both to the precipice they each wanted. Higher and higher as the coils twisted within them.

Finally feeling his own lack of control splintering around him, he slid a finger between the crevice of her cheeks and squeezed while gently stroking the soft tissue beneath. She arched up high and cried out as her body clenched tight around him, milking him of everything he had to give her. His groan erupted from deep inside as his body shuddered and shook with his own orgasm.

Then he collapsed beside her, careful of her arm, and gently tugged her close.

She lifted her fingers to stroke his cheek. "Now I'm tired." She closed her eyes.

He leaned over and kissed her eyelids and whispered, "Sleep. I'll watch over you."

And she believed him. If anything were to happen, Logan would be there for her. She stretched her arm up around him and whispered, "You have been the light that kept me going through all this. But I wanted to tell you that *Alina* means *light.*"

"And that's perfect," he whispered. "Because you're my Alina. You're my light." With her wrapped in his arms, they both fell asleep.

Ready to take the next step of their lives together forever.

Epilogue

HARRISON WAITED FOR Logan to arrive. He was needed for a job. Harrison had been in Mexico for the last two days but had flown in to Houston this morning. It had worked out well, leaving Alina and Logan in Boston. Harrison hoped they'd cemented their relationship. It also gave her a little longer to heal after all she'd been through. He was damn sure Alina would fit right in at the compound. But having Caroline's apartment as a go-between for the moment was even better. At least until Alina had a chance to meet everybody, get to know their people and see how she liked the idea.

Except Logan was not likely to wait.

Some things Logan was possessive about. And this woman was one of them. It amazed Harrison to see how quickly the relationship had solidified between those two. Logan had always had a way with women. Something Harrison didn't. But Logan's relationships had always been lighthearted. This one was different.

That was good. He was happy for his friend.

LOGAN HAD PROMISED to explain all about the compound to Alina so she wasn't completely overwhelmed on arrival. They had arrived at Caroline's place early this morning, helped Alina unpack, and then he would drive Alina out to the compound, so she could meet everyone. He admired her guts. It wouldn't be easy to come into a place like this and be introduced to everyone. They were all good people, but it would still be daunting on her part. She'd been reluctant to accept change, and this would be a huge one.

Harrison was outside in the garage when he heard his name called.

"Harrison, they came around the bend."

He grinned. Everybody was watching. No way they weren't. He crossed his arms and leaned against the open garage bay doors as Logan drove in—in the same car Alina had picked up in the hospital parking lot a few days ago. He could see the two of them talking. Stone and Levi came out and stood beside him. Of course it would be the men first.

Logan grinned sheepishly as he parked the car. A possessive look in his eyes. And pride shone on his face. He got out of the car, and the passenger door opened too.

Harrison took one look at Alina, saw the purple cast and couldn't help but tease her. "Did you really have to beat the poor woman up?"

She slapped her good hand over her mouth to hold back a cry. Then she raced toward him, calling out, "Harrison." She flung herself into his arms.

He had to brace himself to catch her. The little whirlwind didn't weigh more than 110 pounds. He caught her midair and wrapped his arms around her, spinning her into a big hug.

She laughed when he finally put her down and reached up to kiss him on the cheek. "Trust you to get away from all the work," she teased him right back.

He groaned. "I'm not housebroken. Logan is."

She patted him on the cheek. "You're more so than you

would like to admit." Instead of being shy or waiting for
Logan, she turned to the two men beside him. "Well, you're
Stone, and you must be Levi." She held out her left hand to
them. "I'd love to give you a hug as thanks, but I really don't
know you, so maybe a left-handed shake is better."

Levi chuckled. "Hell no." He opened his arms.

She grinned and walked right into them. Logan stood
beside them as she stepped backed. "Thank you so much for
sending these two men to save my life."

Levi said, "If we had known, we would've been there
two days earlier."

Her smile fell away, and shadows deepened her eyes.
"And that would've been much easier on me. But you sent
me my own hero, and for that, I will always be grateful."

Levi winced at the term *hero*.

Harrison chuckled. "Yep, that's what everybody here is,"
he said unhelpfully. "Heroes for Hire. That's the nickname
for the company."

Levi gave him a hard look. "Legendary Security is our
company name."

She turned to face Stone. "Logan's told me so much
about you." She gave him a gentle smile. "And I understand
Lissa has found her own hero with you too."

And damned if Stone didn't blush.

She reached up her arms, and in a move so damn careful,
Stone put his arms around her waist, picked her up and gave
her a hug.

Harrison glanced at Logan to see the surprise on his face
too. "Not only is she an icebreaker but she is definitely a
heartbreaker." He didn't realize he'd said that out loud until
she turned to him.

"Heartbreaker? Me? No." She shook her head and
reached a hand out to Logan. "He's my heartbreaker. My

Heartbreaker Hero." She turned to Logan and kissed him on the cheek. "And if this is Texas, I'm absolutely loving it."

She froze as she caught sight of somebody behind Harrison.

Harrison pivoted and grinned. Alina stepped forward, holding out her left hand again. In a more formal voice, she said, "I'm Alina. You must be Ice."

Ice's cool voice warmed. "Welcome, Alina. From what I've heard, you've been through the grind already."

Tears sparkled on her eyelashes. Alina brushed them away impatiently. "I keep telling myself not to cry anymore. And then it hits at the oddest times."

She turned as several other women came to join them. Lissa wrapped her arms around Stone and said, "You're not alone there. Stone saved me from a kidnapping too."

Ice walked over to stand beside Levi. Then the rest of the gang showed up. Merk with Katina, even Rhodes was here with Sienna. The only ones missing were Flynn and Anna.

Logan asked, "Where's Flynn? Everybody is here but him."

"Not too far from here. He and Anna went into town to sign the purchase documents today," Ice said. "You'll see them tonight."

Alina turned to look at all the couples. "Harrison, where's your girl?"

There were muffled chuckles. He narrowed his gaze to shut them all up and said, "I'm the only sane man here. I'm single and intend to stay that way."

She gave him the sweetest, gentlest smile and said, "Not happening. You're definitely hero material too."

He shook his head and turned to leave. "To hell with that."

"Okay, run then," she called to his back. "But remember, you are a *hero*, and you will find a partner one day."

He turned to face her and give her a hard glare, hoping to cut back some of the sunshine and roses in her voice. Instead, her smile brightened, and she laughed, the musical sound flying easily as it rolled through the garage. How could anybody be upset with so much sunshine? Still, he wasn't giving in without a fight. "You are getting into so much trouble if you say that damn word one more time."

She stepped over the threshold and said, "Hero."

He fisted his hands on his hips and said, "I warned you."

She shoved her face in his and said, "Hero, hero, hero, hero."

He threw his hands in the air. "Logan, control your woman."

Logan responded with a great belly laugh that rippled across the nearby hills. "Hell, no. I haven't found a way to do that yet."

She spun and looked at him. "And you're not going to either."

The other women cheered. They all linked arms together and took Alina inside.

As Ice walked away, she said, "Logan, we're keeping this one."

As Katina passed Harrison, she whispered, "You're next."

He stomped his foot and said, "Forget it. Not happening."

But nobody was listening—maybe not even Harrison.

He gave a loud snort, adding for emphasis, "Never."

This concludes Book 6 of Heroes for Hire: Logan's Light.

Book 7 is available.

Harrison's Heart: Heroes for Hire, Book 7

Buy this book at your favorite vendor.

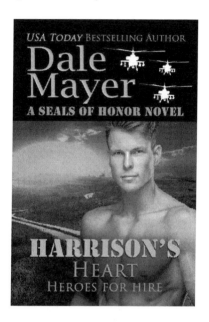

Welcome to *Harrison's Heart*, book 7 in *Heroes for Hire*, reconnecting readers with the unforgettable men from *SEALs of Honor* in a new series of action-packed, page turning romantic suspense that fans have come to expect from USA TODAY Bestselling author Dale Mayer.

When a call for help comes from Ice's father, Harrison steps up. A senator has been shot, his wife beaten and his kids are in the wind. It's up to Harrison to find the answers everyone is looking for.

Including finding the senator's ex-military and pissed at the world daughter. Only she doesn't want anything to do with him.

Zoe is on a mission. There's no room in her world for heroes – especially not Harrison. But he won't take no for an answer. Only Zoe has angered the wrong people, and they won't stop until they put an end to her meddling or better yet – to her.

With so much going on, Harrison struggles to pull the pieces together – before their world is completely blown apart – permanently.

Heroes for Hire Series

Levi's Legend: Heroes for Hire, Book 1

Stone's Surrender: Heroes for Hire, Book 2

Merk's Mistake: Heroes for Hire, Book 3

Rhodes's Reward: Heroes for Hire, Book 4

Flynn's Firecracker: Heroes for Hire, Book 5

Logan's Light: Heroes for Hire, Book 6

Harrison's Heart: Heroes for Hire, Book 7

Saul's Sweetheart: Heroes for Hire, Book 8

Dakata's Delight: Heroes for Hire, Book 9

Michael's Mercy: Heroes for Hire, Book 10

Jarrod's Jewel: Heroes for Hire, Book 11

Author's Note

Thanks for reading. By now many of you have read my explanation of how I love to see **Star Ratings.** The only catch is that we as authors have no idea what you think of a book if it's not reviewed. And yes, **every book in a series needs reviews**. All it takes is a little as two words: Fun Story. Yep, that's all. So, if you enjoyed reading, please take a second to let others know you enjoyed.

For those of you who have not read a previous book and have no idea why we authors keep asking you as a reader to take a few minutes to leave even a two word review, here's more explanation of reviews in this crazy business.

Reviews (not just ratings) help authors qualify for advertising opportunities and help other readers make purchasing decisions. Without *triple digit* reviews, an author may miss out on valuable advertising opportunities. And with only "star ratings" the author has little chance of participating in certain promotions. Which means fewer sales offered to my favorite readers!

Another reason to take a minute and leave a review is that often a **few kind words left in a review can make a huge difference to an author and their muse.** Recently new to reviewing fans have left a few words after reading a similar letter and they were tonic to tired muse! LOL Seriously. Star ratings simply do not have the same impact to thank or encourage an author when the writing gets tough.

So please consider taking a moment to write even a handful of words. Writing a review only takes a few minutes of your time. It doesn't have to be a lengthy book report, just a few words expressing what you enjoyed most about the story. Here are a few tips of how to leave a review.

Please continue to rate the books as you read, but take an extra moment and pop over to the review section and leave a few words too!

Most of all – **Thank you** for reading. I look forward to hearing from you.

I love to hear from readers, and you can contact me at my website: www.dalemayer.com or at my Facebook author page. To be informed of new releases and special offers, sign up for my newsletter or follow me on BookBub. And if you are interested in joining Dale Mayer's Fan Club, here is the Facebook sign up page.
facebook.com/groups/402384989872660

Cheers,
Dale Mayer

Your Free Book Awaits!

KILL OR BE KILLED

Part of an elite SEAL team, Mason takes on the dangerous jobs no one else wants to do – or can do. When he's on a mission, he's focused and dedicated. When he's not, he plays as hard as he fights.

Until he meets a woman he can't have but can't forget. Software developer, Tesla lost her brother in combat and has no intention of getting close to someone else in the military. Determined to save other US soldiers from a similar fate, she's created a program that could save lives. But other countries know about the program, and they won't stop until they get it – and get her.

Time is running out ... For her ... For him ... For them ...

DOWNLOAD a ***complimentary*** copy of MASON? Just tell me where to send it!

http://dalemayer.com/sealsmason/

Touched by Death

Adult RS/thriller

Get this book at your favorite vendor.

Death had touched anthropologist Jade Hansen in Haiti once before, costing her an unborn child and perhaps her very sanity.

A year later, determined to face her own issues, she returns to Haiti with a mortuary team to recover the bodies of an American family from a mass grave. Visiting his brother after the quake, independent contractor Dane Carter puts his life on hold to help the sleepy town of Jacmel rebuild. But he finds it hard to like his brother's pregnant wife or her family. He wants to go home, until he meets Jade – and realizes what's missing in his own life. When the mortuary team begins work, it's as if malevolence has been released from the earth. Instead of laying her ghosts to rest, Jade finds herself confronting death and terror again.

And the man who unexpectedly awakens her heart – is right in the middle of it all.

By Death Series

Touched by Death – Part 1
Touched by Death – Part 2
Touched by Death – Parts 1&2
Haunted by Death
Chilled by Death
By Death Books 1–3

Vampire in Denial

This is book 1 of the Family Blood Ties Saga

Get this book at your favorite vendor.

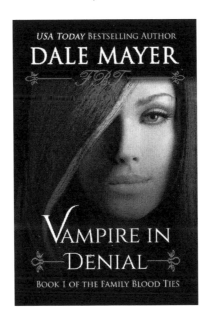

Blood doesn't just make her who she is...it also makes her what she is.

Like being a sixteen-year-old vampire isn't hard enough, Tessa's throwback human genes make her an outcast among her relatives. But try as she might, she can't get a handle on the vampire lifestyle and all the...blood.

Turning her back on the vamp world, she embraces the human teenage lifestyle—high school, peer pressure and finding a boyfriend. Jared manages to stir something in her blood. He's smart and fun and oh, so cute. But Tessa's dream of a having the perfect boyfriend turns into a nightmare when vampires attack the movie theatre and kidnap her date.

Once again, Tessa finds herself torn between the human world and the vampire one. Will blood own out? Can she make peace with who she is as well as what?

Warning: This book ends with a cliffhanger! Book 2 picks up where this book ends.

Family Blood Ties Series

Vampire in Denial

Vampire in Distress

Vampire in Design

Vampire in Deceit

Vampire in Defiance

Vampire in Conflict

Vampire in Chaos

Vampire in Crisis

Vampire in Control

Vampire in Charge

Family Blood Ties Set 1–3

Family Blood Ties Set 1–5

Family Blood Ties Set 4–6

Family Blood Ties Set 7–9

Sian's Solution – A Family Blood Ties Short Story

Broken Protocols

Get this book at your favorite vendor.

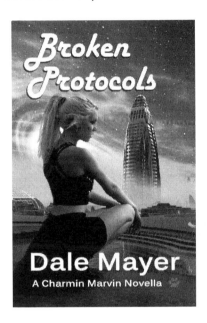

Dani's been through a year of hell...

Just as it's getting better, she's tossed forward through time with her orange Persian cat, Charmin Marvin, clutched in her arms. They're dropped into a few centuries into the future. There's nothing she can do to stop it, and it's impossible to go back.

And then it gets worse...

A year of government regulation is easing, and Levi Blackburn is feeling back in control. If he can keep his reckless brother in check, everything will be perfect. But while he's been protecting Milo from the government, Milo's been busy working on a present for him…

The present is Dani, only she comes with a snarky cat who suddenly starts talking…and doesn't know when to shut up.

In an age where breaking protocols have severe consequences, things go wrong, putting them all in danger…

Charmin Marvin Romantic Comedy Series

Broken Protocols

Broken Protocols 2

Broken Protocols 3

Broken Protocols 3.5

Broken Protocols 1-3

About the Author

Dale Mayer is a USA Today bestselling author best known for her Psychic Visions and Family Blood Ties series. Her contemporary romances are raw and full of passion and emotion (Second Chances, SKIN), her thrillers will keep you guessing (By Death series), and her romantic comedies will keep you giggling (It's a Dog's Life and Charmin Marvin Romantic Comedy series).

She honors the stories that come to her – and some of them are crazy and break all the rules and cross multiple genres!

To go with her fiction, she also writes nonfiction in many different fields with books available on resume writing, companion gardening and the US mortgage system. She has recently published her Career Essentials Series. All her books are available in print and ebook format.

Connect with Dale Mayer Online

Dale's Website – www.dalemayer.com
Twitter – @DaleMayer
Facebook – facebook.com/DaleMayer.author
BookBub – bookbub.com/authors/dale-mayer

Also by Dale Mayer

Published Adult Books:

Psychic Vision Series
Tuesday's Child

Hide'n Go Seek

Maddy's Floor

Garden of Sorrow

Knock, Knock…

Rare Find

Eyes to the Soul

Now You See Her

Shattered

Into the Abyss

Seeds of Malice

Eye of the Falcon

Psychic Visions Books 1–3

Psychic Visions Books 4–6

Psychic Visions Books 7–9

By Death Series
Touched by Death – Part 1

Touched by Death – Part 2

Touched by Death – Parts 1&2

Haunted by Death

Chilled by Death

By Death Books 1–3

Second Chances…at Love Series

Second Chances – Part 1

Second Chances – Part 2

Second Chances – complete book (Parts 1 & 2)

Charmin Marvin Romantic Comedy Series

Broken Protocols

Broken Protocols 2

Broken Protocols 3

Broken Protocols 3.5

Broken Protocols 1-3

Broken and… Mending

Skin

Scars

Scales (of Justice)

Broken but… Mending 1-3

Glory

Genesis

Tori

Celeste

Glory Trilogy

Biker Blues

Biker Blues: Morgan, Part 1

Biker Blues: Morgan, Part 2

Biker Blues: Morgan, Part 3

Biker Baby Blues: Morgan, Part 4

Biker Blues: Morgan, Full Set

Biker Blues: Salvation, Part 1

Biker Blues: Salvation, Part 2

Biker Blues: Salvation, Part 3

Biker Blues: Salvation, Full Set

SEALs of Honor

Mason: SEALs of Honor, Book 1

Hawk: SEALs of Honor, Book 2

Dane: SEALs of Honor, Book 3

Swede: SEALs of Honor, Book 4

Shadow: SEALs of Honor, Book 5

Cooper: SEALs of Honor, Book 6

Markus: SEALs of Honor, Book 7

Evan: SEALs of Honor, Book 8

Mason's Wish: SEALs of Honor, Book 9

Chase: SEALs of Honor, Book 10

Brett: SEALs of Honor, Book 11

Devlin: SEALs of Honor, Book 12

Easton: SEALs of Honor, Book 13

SEALs of Honor, Books 1–3

SEALs of Honor, Books 4–6

SEALs of Honor, Books 7–10

Heroes for Hire

Levi's Legend: Heroes for Hire, Book 1

Stone's Surrender: Heroes for Hire, Book 2

Merk's Mistake: Heroes for Hire, Book 3

Rhodes's Reward: Heroes for Hire, Book 4

Flynn's Firecracker: Heroes for Hire, Book 5

Logan's Light: Heroes for Hire, Book 6

Harrison's Heart: Heroes for Hire, Book 7

Saul's Sweetheart: Heroes for Hire, Book 8

Dakata's Delight: Heroes for Hire, Book 9

Michael's Mercy: Heroes for Hire, Book 10

Jarrod's Jewel: Heroes for Hire, Book 11

Collections

Dare to Be You…

Dare to Love…

Dare to be Strong…

RomanceX3

Standalone Novellas

It's a Dog's Life

Riana's Revenge

Published Young Adult Books:

Family Blood Ties Series

Vampire in Denial

Vampire in Distress

Vampire in Design

Vampire in Deceit

Vampire in Defiance

Vampire in Conflict

Vampire in Chaos

Vampire in Crisis

Vampire in Control

Vampire in Charge

Family Blood Ties Set 1–3

Family Blood Ties Set 1–5

Family Blood Ties Set 4–6

Family Blood Ties Set 7–9

Sian's Solution – A Family Blood Ties Short Story

Design series

Dangerous Designs

Deadly Designs

Darkest Designs

Design Series Trilogy

Standalone

In Cassie's Corner

Gem Stone (a Gemma Stone Mystery)

Time Thieves

Published Non-Fiction Books:

Career Essentials

Career Essentials: The Résumé

Career Essentials: The Cover Letter

Career Essentials: The Interview

Career Essentials: 3 in 1

79736108R00127

Made in the USA
Lexington, KY
25 January 2018